RUMORS
A Farce

by

Neil Simon

S A M U E L   F R E N C H ,   I N C.
45 WEST 25th STREET   NEW YORK 10010
7623 SUNSET BOULEVARD   HOLLYWOOD 90046
LONDON   TORONTO

IMPORTANT BILLING AND CREDIT REQUIREMENTS

All producers of RUMORS *must* give credit to the Author of the Play in all programs distributed in connection with performances of the Play and in all instances in which the title of the Play appears for purposes of advertising, publicizing or otherwise exploiting the Play and/or a production. The name of the Author *must* also appear on a separate line, on which no other name appears, immediately following the title, and *must* appear in size of type not less than fifty percent the size of the title type.

MANDATORY MUSIC ROYALTY

Producers are required to use the song "La Bamba" in productions of RUMORS. Amateur Music Royalty is $6.00/ performance, or $30/week—whichever is less. Stock Music Royalty is $5.50 per performance or $27.50/week—whichever is less. PLEASE NOTE: This does not include rights to use any specific recording of the song, such as that by Richie Valens.

Rumors by Neil Simon was produced by The Old Globe Theatre in San Diego, California. It opened on September 22, 1988 with the following cast:

CHRIS GORMAN .... Christine Baranski
KEN   GORMAN.................... Mark Nelson
CLAIRE GANZ .... Jessica Walter
LENNY   GANZ...................... Ron Leibman
ERNIE   CUSACK.................. Andre Gregory
COOKIE CUSACK............. Joyce Van Patten
GLENN COOPER.................... Ken Howard
CASSIE   COOPER...................... Lisa Banes
OFFICER WELCH................ Charles Brown
OFFICER   PUDNEY............. Cynthia Darlow

Rumors was directed by Gene Saks. The set was designed by Tony Straiges, the lighting was designed by Tharon Musser and the costumes were designed by Joseph G. Aulisi. Douglas Pagliotti was the production stage manager.

Rumors by Neil Simon was subsequently produced by Emanuel Azenberg at the Broadhurst Theatre in New York City. It opened November 17, 1988, with the following cast:

CHRIS GORMAN............Christine Baranski
KEN   GORMAN......................Mark Nelson
CLAIRE GANZ ....Jessica Walter
LENNY   GANZ...................... Ron Leibman
ERNIE   CUSACK...................Andre Gregory
COOKIE CUSACK............... Joyce Van Patten
GLENN COOPER....................Ken Howard
CASSIE   COOPER...................... Lisa Banes
OFFICER WELCH.................Charles Brown
OFFICER   PUDNEY...............Cynthia Darlow

Rumors was directed by Gene Saks. The set was designed by Tony Straiges, the lighting was designed by Tharon Musser, the costumes were designed by Joseph G. Aulisi, and the sound was designed by Tom Morse. Peter Lawrence was the production stage manager.

CHARACTERS

Chris Gorman
Ken Gorman
Claire Ganz
Lenny Ganz
Ernie Cusack
Cookie Cusack
Glenn Cooper
Cassie Cooper
Officer Welch
Officer Pudney

PLACE: Sneden's Landing, New York

TIME: The present

ACT I

SCENE: A large, tastefully renovated, Victorian house in Sneden's Landing, New York, about forty minutes from the city. Despite its age and gingerbread exterior, the interior is modern, monochromatic and sparkling clean. A nice combination.

An entrance doorway at Upstage Right leads onto an open vestibule. To the right of the door is a powder room. One step down, is the large and comfortable living room. The color is predominately white.

There are two furniture groupings in the living room. Stage Right are a love seat and two chairs. Upstage of the love seat and near the powder room door is a table and a telephone with a long cord. Center Stage is a large sofa and coffee table. Two chairs Stage Left are part of a grouping with the sofa. On the Stage Left wall is a mirror in an ornate frame. Against the Upstage wall are a well-stocked bar and a stereo system enclosed in a gorgeous cabinet. Between these two pieces is a closed door leading to the cellar.

From the living room, a curved staircase leads to a landing and two doors; each to a bedroom. On the landing is a railed bannister. At the Stage Left end of the second-floor landing is an archway leading to a hallway and more bedrooms. Downstage of this archway is an extension of the balcony which can be used as a playing area.

Through the living room, at Left, double doors lead into a dining room and then, the kitchen. A huge window

9

above the front door looks out onto a wooded backyard. A large window in the Stage Right wall overlooks a yard and the driveway beyond. Headlights of approaching cars may be seen through this window.

AT RISE: It is about eight-thirty at night on a pleasant evening in May.
CHRIS GORMAN, an attractive woman, mid-thirties, paces anxiously back and forth, looking at her watch, biting her nails. SHE is elegantly dressed in a designer gown. SHE looks at the phone, then at her watch again. SHE seems to make a decision and crosses to the cigarette box on the coffee table. SHE takes out a cigarette, then puts it back.

CHRIS. Oh, my God!

(Suddenly, Charley's bedroom door opens on the second landing and KEN GORMAN, about forty, dressed smartly in a tuxedo but looking flushed and excited, comes out to the rail. THEY BOTH speak rapidly.)

KEN. Did he call yet?
CHRIS. Wouldn't I have yelled up?
KEN. Call him again.
CHRIS. I called him twice. They're looking for him . . . How is he?
KEN. I'm not sure. He's bleeding like crazy.
CHRIS. Oh, my God!
KEN. It's all over the room. I don't know why people decorate in white ... If he doesn't call in two minutes, call the hospital.
CHRIS. I'm going to have to have a cigarette, Ken.

KEN. After eighteen months, the hell you are. Hold onto yourself, will you?

(*HE rushes back in, closes the door behind him. SHE returns to pacing.*)

CHRIS. I can't believe this is happening. (*SHE crosses to the cigarette box. The PHONE rings.*) Oh, God! (*SHE calls out.*) Ken, the phone is ringing. (*But HE's gone. SHE crosses to phone and picks it up.*) Hello? Dr. Dudley? . . . Oh, Dr. Dudley, I'm so glad it's you. Your service said you were at the theatre.

(*Charley's bedroom door opens, KEN looks out.*)

KEN. Is that the doctor?
CHRIS. (*Into phone.*) I never would have bothered you, but this is an emergency.
KEN. Is that the doctor?
CHRIS. (*Into the phone.*) I'm Chris Gorman. My husband Ken and I are good friends of Charley Brock's.
KEN. Is that the doctor?
CHRIS. (*Turns, holds phone, yells at Ken.*) *It's the doctor! It's the doctor!*
KEN. (*Angrily.*) Why didn't you say so? (*HE goes back in, closes the door.*)
CHRIS. (*Into the phone.*) Dr. Dudley, I'm afraid there's been an accident ... I would have called my own doctor, but my husband is a lawyer and under the circumstances, he thought it better to have Charley's own physician ... Well, we just arrived here at Charley's house about ten minutes ago, and as we were getting out of our car, we suddenly heard this enormous —

(KEN suddenly comes out of the bedroom)

KEN. Don't say anything!

CHRIS. *(To Ken.)* What?

KEN. Don't tell him what happened!

CHRIS. Don't tell him?

KEN. Just do what I say.

CHRIS. What about Charley?

KEN. He's all right. It's just a powder burn. Don't tell him about the gunshot.

CHRIS. But they got the doctor out of the theatre.

KEN. Tell him he tripped down the stairs and banged his head. He's all right.

CHRIS. But what about the blood?

KEN. The bullet went through his ear lobe. It's nothing. I don't want him to know.

CHRIS. But I already said we were getting out of the car and we suddenly heard an enormous – what? What did we hear?

KEN. *(Coming downstairs.)* We heard ...

CHRIS. *(Into phone.)* Just a minute, doctor.

KEN. *(Thinks, coming downstairs.)* We heard ... we heard ... we heard ... an enormous – *thud!*

CHRIS. Thud?

KEN. When he tripped down the stairs.

CHRIS. Good. Good. That's good. *(Into phone.)* Dr. Dudley? I'm sorry. I was talking to my husband. Well, we heard this enormous *thud!* It seemed Charley tripped going up the stairs.

KEN. *Down!* Down the stairs.

CHRIS. *Down* the stairs. But he's all right.

KEN. He's sitting up in bed. He'll call him in the morning.

CHRIS. He's sitting up in bed. He'll call him in the morning.

KEN. *You!*

CHRIS. *You!* He'll call *you* in the morning.

KEN. You're very sorry you disturbed him.

CHRIS. I'm very sorry I disturbed you.

KEN. But he's really fine.

CHRIS. But he's really fine.

KEN. Thank you. Goodbye.

CHRIS. (*To Ken.*) Where are you going?

KEN. *Him! Him!* Thank him and say goodbye.

CHRIS. Oh. (*Into phone.*) Thank you and goodbye, Doctor ... What? ... Just a minute. (*To Ken as HE goes upstairs.*) Any dizziness?

KEN. No. No dizziness.

CHRIS. (*Into phone.*) No. No dizziness ... What? (*To Ken.*) Can he move his limbs?

KEN. (*Irritated.*) Yes! He can move everything. Get off the phone.

CHRIS. (*Yells at Ken.*) They got him out of *Phantom of the Opera.* (*Into phone.*) Yes, he can move everything ... What? (*To Ken.*) Any slurring of the speech?

KEN. NO! NO SLURRING OF THE SPEECH.

CHRIS. (*To Ken.*) Don't yell at me. He'll hear it. (*Into phone.*) No. No slurring of the speech.

KEN. I've got to get back to Charley. (*KEN starts to back into Charley's room.*)

CHRIS. (*Into phone.*) Any what? (*To Ken.*) Any ringing of the ears?

KEN. I can't believe this ... No. Tell him no.

CHRIS. (*Into phone.*) Yes. A little ringing in the ears.

KEN. I told you to say no.

CHRIS. It sounds more believable to have ringing.

KEN. Jesus!

CHRIS. (*Into phone.*) Who? His wife? Myra? ... Yes. Myra's here.

KEN. (*Rushing downstairs.*) She's *not* here. Don't tell him she's here. He'll want to speak to her.

CHRIS. (*Into phone.*) Dr. Dudley? My mistake. She's not here. I thought she was but she wasn't.

KEN. She just stepped out. She'll be back in a minute.

CHRIS. (*Into phone.*) She just stepped back. She'll be out in a minute. Yes. I'll tell her to call.

(*KEN goes back upstairs.*)

CHRIS. ... Okay, thank you, Dr. Diddley ... Dudley. Enjoy the show. Ken and I saw it, we loved it ... Especially the second act. Who's playing the Phantom tonight?

KEN. Are you going to review the whole goddam show? (*KEN goes back into Charley's room.*)

CHRIS. Oh, Charley's calling me. (*Calls out.*) Just a minute, Charley. (*Into phone.*) He sounds a lot better. I have to go. Yes, Doctor, I will. (*SHE hangs up, furious at Ken.*) Don't you *ever* do that to me again. He must suspect something. I didn't get his name right once.

KEN. (*Coming out of the bedroom.*) If anyone calls again, don't answer it. (*HE starts to go into the bedroom.*)

CHRIS. Then why did you tell me to answer that one?

KEN. Because I thought the bullet went through his head, not his ear lobe. Fix me a double vodka, I left Charley standing in the shower.

CHRIS. If he drowns, you're making that call.

(*KEN goes into the bedroom.*)

CHRIS. I don't know why we're always the first ones here. (*SHE fixes the vodka.*) Never came late once in our lives. Someone else could have dealt with all this. (*SHE goes to the cigarette box once more. the DOORBELL rings. SHE jumps.*) Oh, SHIT! Shit shit shit shit!

(*The upstairs door opens, KEN comes out.*)

KEN. Who's that? Who is that?
CHRIS. Am I near the door? Do you see people in here? You think I'm on roller skates?
KEN. Let me think a minute.
CHRIS. Take your time because I don't answer doors. I only speak to Dr. Dudley.
KEN. All right. It's got to be Lenny or Ernie, one of the others. We've got to open the door.
CHRIS. You've got arms, reach down.
KEN. I've got to dry Charley off and bandage his ear. Don't tell them what happened. I need a few minutes to figure this out. Can't you stall them?
CHRIS. His best friends are coming to his tenth anniversary, his wife isn't here, he shoots himself in the ear lobe and I'm supposed to make small talk when they come in?
KEN. Attempted suicide is a criminal offense, not to mention a pretty ugly scandal. Charley's Deputy Mayor of New York. He's my client and my best friend, I've got to protect him, don't I? Just play the hostess for a few minutes until I figure out how to handle this.

(The DOORBELL rings again.)

CHRIS. Play the hostess? There's no food out, there's no ice in the bucket. Where's the help? Where's the cheese dip? Where's Myra? What am I supposed to do till you get back, play charades? I'm lucky I can still speak English.

KEN. You're a lawyer yourself, can't you figure out something to say?

CHRIS. Contracts! I draw up legal publishing contracts. If someone walks in the door and wants to make a deal, I CAN HANDLE THAT!!

KEN. Take it easy. Calm down. I'll be right back.

(The DOORBELL rings again.)

CHRIS. Put some slippers on Charley and tell him to answer it.

KEN. *(Yells.)* Would you relax? Drink my vodka.

CHRIS. Why is a vodka better than two puffs of a cigarette?

KEN. Because they know you quit and if they see smoke in here, they'll know something is wrong.

CHRIS. You mean falling at their feet is going to look better?

(The DOORBELL rings impatiently.
KEN runs into the bedroom and closes the door. CHRIS crosses to the front door. SHE opens it.
CLAIRE rushes into the living room. SHE's an attractive woman in an evening gown. SHE holds a handkerchief to the side of her mouth, a purse in the other hand.)

CHRIS. Claire, darling, you look beautiful. Where's Lenny?

CLAIRE. (*Coming in.*) In the car. We had an accident. Brand new BMW, two days old, the side door is smashed in. Don't tell Charley and Myra, I don't want to ruin tonight for them. (*SHE crosses to mirror and looks at her face.*)

CHRIS. Oh, my God! Are you hurt?

CLAIRE. My lip is swelling up. (*Looks in the wall mirror.*) Oh, Jesus, I look like a trumpet player.

CHRIS. Where's Lenny?

CLAIRE. He's coming. He's walking slowly, he's got whiplash. His seat belt went right around his neck, and pulled him straight up. I left him dangling.

CHRIS. Oh, sweetheart, I'm sorry. Is there anything I can do?

CLAIRE. Just don't tell Myra. This party means so much to her.

(*LENNY comes in through the front door. He's wearing a tuxedo, one hand holds the back of his neck, in the other arm HE has a gift box from Steuben's.*)

LENNY. (*In pain, but smiles. His neck is stiff.*) Hi, Charley! Hi, Myra! We're here, kids.

CHRIS. They're upstairs, Lenny.

LENNY. (*To Chris.*) Did she tell you what happened? Some stupid bastard shoots out of his garage like a Polaris rocket. I've got four doors on one side of the car now.

CHRIS. How does your neck feel?

LENNY. Stretched out, over to one side. I look like a Modigliani painting. (*HE crosses to the phone.*)

CHRIS. Do you want a drink?

LENNY. I don't think I could swallow past my shoulders.

CLAIRE. Of all nights to happen.

LENNY. Here's their gift. Steuben glass. (*HE shakes box. We hear broken glass RATTLE.*) If someone brings them a bottle of glue, they'll have a nice gift. (*HE starts to dial, carefully.*)

CLAIRE. (*Looks at her mouth in a hand mirror.*) I could have lost the tip of my tongue. I'd be speaking Gaelic the rest of my life.

LENNY. (*Waiting for his call.*) A brand new, spotless car, never touched by human hands. Buffed and polished by German women in Munich and now it looks like a war memorial. (*Into phone.*) Hello? This is Leonard Ganz. Is Dr. Dudley there, please?

CHRIS. Dr. Dudley?

LENNY. (*Into phone.*) Yes, it is. I have a whiplash injury ... I see ... Do you know what theatre he's in?

CHRIS. Oh, God, I need a cigarette so badly.

LENNY. Could you? It's important. I'm at – (*HE looks at phone.*) 914-473-2261 ... Thank you very much. (*HE hangs up.*)

CLAIRE. I've got to settle my stomach. Is there anything to eat? Some canapes or something?

CHRIS. Gee, I don't see anything.

CLAIRE. No canapes? Where's the cook, Mai Li? She makes great canapes.

CHRIS. Mai Li? I didn't see her. I think she's off this week.

CLAIRE. The week of their anniversary party?

CHRIS. I think she had to go back to Japan. Her mother was sick.

CLAIRE. Mai Li is Chinese.

CHRIS. I know. Her mother was visiting Japan.

LENNY. (*Still bracing his neck.*) I can only look up. I hope tall people are coming to this party ... Where's Ken?

CHRIS. Ken? He went to the bathroom.

LENNY. And where's Charley and Myra?

CHRIS. They're still getting dressed.

LENNY. They're not ready? We had a *car* accident and we're on time.

CLAIRE. (*Looks in hand mirror again.*) My lip is getting gigantic. I don't think I have enough lipstick to cover it.

LENNY. No nuts or pretzels? I didn't even have lunch today. Three goddam audits with the IRS on an empty stomach. (*HE gets up.*) Claire, get me a Diet Coke, please, and something to munch on. (*HE starts for the stairs.*)

CHRIS. Where are you going?

LENNY. To the john. I haven't had a chance to do that either.

CHRIS. There's a guest powder room down here.

LENNY. Isn't Ken using that?

CHRIS. No, he's using the one in the guest bedroom upstairs.

LENNY. (*Pointing to the powder room.*) Why didn't he use this one?

CHRIS. I don't know. He said he had to go badly and he ran upstairs.

LENNY. If he had to go so bad, the one downstairs is closer.

CHRIS. You know how it is when you have to go badly. You don't want to stop running.

LENNY. But this is a shorter run.

CLAIRE. Lenny, it's not an Olympic event. Why don't you just go?

LENNY. That's why they build guest bathrooms. (*Starts for powder room.*) If Dr. Dudley calls, I'll be right out. (*HE goes into powder room and closes door.*)

CHRIS. Claire, we have to talk.

CLAIRE. (*Goes to sit near Chris.*) What is it?

CHRIS. I'm coming apart at the seams.

CLAIRE. Your dress?

CHRIS. No, my nerves. I think I'm going to crack.

CLAIRE. I can see. (*Taking Chris's hand.*) Your hands are like ice. Something is going on here, isn't it?

CHRIS. Oh, God, you're so smart. You're so quick to see things.

CLAIRE. You're scaring me, Chris. Tell me what's happening.

CHRIS. Well, all right. Ken and I arrived here about ten minutes ago, when suddenly we heard this enormous ...

(*Charley's bedroom door opens. KEN steps out.*)

KEN. Hey, Claire! You look lovely.

CHRIS. Yes! I was just telling her that. She looks enormously well, doesn't she? (*To Claire.*) Isn't that the dress you wore for Cerebral Palsy?

CLAIRE. No. I got this for Sickle Cell. Hi, Ken.

KEN. Where's Lenny?

CLAIRE. He's in the john. Where's Charley and Myra?

CHRIS. (*To Ken.*) Still getting dressed?

KEN. Yes. Still getting dressed ... How's the new BMW? Is Len happy with it?

CLAIRE. Delirious.

KEN. Did he get the new featues he asked for?

CLAIRE. More than he asked for.

KEN. Great.

CLAIRE. Are you through in the bathroom, Ken? I have to go myself. (*SHE starts for the stairs.*)

KEN. I think Myra's in there.

CLAIRE. Then I'll use Mai Li's bathroom. Call me if she gets back from Japan. (*SHE goes into the kitchen.*)

KEN. (*Waves his arms at Chris.*) Up here! Quick!

(*CHRIS rushes up the stairs.*)

KEN. Hurry up!

(*Breathlessly, SHE gets there.*)

KEN. What did you tell her?

CHRIS. I can't remember.

KEN. You can't remember?

CHRIS. I couldn't follow it, I was talking so fast. Why can't we tell them the truth? They're going to find out anyway.

KEN. I don't *know* the truth yet. Charley is still mumbling. Now go inside. He wants to see you.

CHRIS. See *me?* Why does he want to see me?

KEN. He's crying like a baby. I can't stop him. He needs a woman.

CHRIS. ... To do what?

KEN. To cry on. I can reason with him but I can't comfort him. Let him cry on your shoulder for two minutes, for crise sakes.

CHRIS. (*Starting into Charley's room*) Is he still bleeding? I paid twelve hundred dollars for this dress.

(*SHE goes in and closes the door just as LENNY comes out of the powder room.*)

KEN. Oh, hi, Len!

LENNY. (*Looks up, winces.*) Oh, Jesus. (*HE grabs his neck.*) Hi, Ken. Did you hear about the BMW?

KEN. Yeah. Congratulations. Excuse me. (*HE turns to go.*)

LENNY. Where are you going?

KEN. To the john.

LENNY. Didn't you just go?

KEN. ... Yes. But not enough. Be right with you.

(*HE goes into the guest room, just as CLAIRE comes out of the kitchen with a bag of pretzels, unopened.*)

CLAIRE. This is very weird.

LENNY. Give me the pretzels. (*HE grabs the bag.*)

CLAIRE. (*Pours two Cokes.*) There's plenty of food in the kitchen, but nothing's cooked.

LENNY. Why didn't you open this first? (*HE struggles with the bag.*)

CLAIRE. There's a duck, roast ham, smoked turkey, all defrosting on the table. There's pasta sitting in a pot with no water.

(*LENNY can't open the bag. HE bites into it.*)

CLAIRE. Everything's ready to go, but no one's there to start it. Doesn't that seem strange to you?

LENNY. Not as strange as him peeing twice in a row ... Have you got something sharp, a nail file or something?

CLAIRE. Chris started to tell me something and then she clammed up.

LENNY. The door on my BMW opened like tissue paper but this thing is like steel.

CLAIRE. Her hands were as cold as ice. She couldn't look me straight in the eye.

LENNY. This would be a safe place to keep your jewelry!! (*HE tries one last time to open it, then throws it away.*) Goddammit!!

CLAIRE. And why are they taking so long to get dressed? What is that about, heh?

LENNY. What are you so damn suspicious for? Give the people a chance to come down.

CLAIRE. Oh, you don't notice anything is wrong?

LENNY. Yes, I noticed. I noticed the towels in the bathroom were piled up on the sink and not on the rack. I noticed there's only a sheet-and-a-half left on the toilet paper. I think it's sloppy, but not a scandal.

CLAIRE. Really? Well, I'm not so sure I'd rule out a scandal. (*SHE walks away from him.*)

LENNY. You think I don't know what you're talking about? I hear what's going on. I hear gossip, I hear rumors and I won't listen to that crap, you understand. He is my friend, she is the wife of my friend.

CLAIRE. Fine! Okay, then forget it.

LENNY. I don't listen to filth and garbage about my friends.

CLAIRE. I said forget it.

LENNY. (*Looks at her.*) ... All right. Come here. (*HE walks to the extreme Downstage Right corner of the living room.*)

CLAIRE. What's wrong with here?

LENNY. They could hear us there. Here is better. Will you come here!

(*SHE crosses to him. HE looks around, then to her.*)

LENNY. It's not good.
CLAIRE. What's not good?
LENNY. What I heard.
CLAIRE. What did you hear?
LENNY. Will you lower your voice?
CLAIRE. Why? We haven't said anything yet.
LENNY. All right. There's talk going around about Myra and— This hurts me. Stand on my other side. I can't turn.

(*SHE turns with her back to him. HE moves to her other side.*)

LENNY. There's talk going around about Myra and Charley. Only no one will tell it to my face because they know I won't listen.
CLAIRE. I'll listen. Tell it to my face.
LENNY. Why would you want to hear things about our best friends? He's my best client. He trusts me. Not just about investments and taxes, but personal things.
CLAIRE. I don't do his taxes, what's the rumors?
LENNY. Jesus, you won't be satisfied till you hear, will you?
CLAIRE. I won't even *sleep* with you until I hear. What's the rumors?
LENNY. ... All right. Your friend Myra upstairs is having herself a little thing, okay?
CLAIRE. What kind of thing?

LENNY. Do I have to spell it out? A thing. A guy. A man. A fella. A kid. An affair. She's doing something with someone on the sly somewhere and it's not with Charley. Okay?

CLAIRE. You don't know that. You only heard it. You haven't seen it.

LENNY. Of course I haven't seen it. You think they invite me to come along? What's wrong with you?

CLAIRE. You are so naive, it's incredible. Get real, Lenny. Myra's not having anything with anybody. Your friend, Charley, however, is running up a hell of a motel bill.

LENNY. Charley? My friend, Charley? No way. Not a chance. He wouldn't even look at another woman.

CLAIRE. He may not be looking at her, but he's screwing her.

LENNY. Will you lower your voice! ... Where did you hear this?

CLAIRE. Someone at the tennis club told me.

LENNY. *Our* tennis club?

CLAIRE. What is it, a sacred temple? People gossip there.

LENNY. Christ! Bunch of hypocrites. Sit around in their brand-new Nikes and Reeboks destroying people's lives ... Who told you this?

CLAIRE. I'm not going to tell you because you don't like this person anyway.

LENNY. What's the difference if I like them or not? Who told you?

CLAIRE. Carole Newman.

LENNY. CAROLE NEWMAN?? I knew it, I knew it. I *hate* that goddam woman. She's got a mouth big enough to swallow a can of tennis balls.

(*The guest room door opens and KEN steps out onto the landing.*)

KEN. (Affably.) How you two doing?
LENNY. Hey! Just fine, Ken.
KEN. Had anything to eat yet?
LENNY. Just a plastic bag.
KEN. Great! Be right back.

(*KEN goes into Charley's bedroom and closes the door.*)

LENNY. Wasn't it Carole Newman who spread the other rumor?
CLAIRE. What other rumor?
LENNY. The rumor that you and I were breaking up.
CLAIRE. No. It wasn't Carole Newman.
LENNY. It wasn't? Then who was it?
CLAIRE. It was me.
LENNY. *You* started the rumor?
CLAIRE. Me, you, the both of us. When we were thinking about separating, didn't we go around telling everyone?
LENNY. We told friends. That bitch told strangers.
CLAIRE. Hey! Hey! Do *not* call Carole Newman a bitch to my face. Besides, Carole Newman didn't start the rumor about Charley. Someone else at the club told her. (*SHE walks to the bar.*)
LENNY. Who was the one who told her?
CLAIRE. Harold Green.
LENNY. Harold Green? Who the hell is Harold Green?
CLAIRE. He's a new member. He was just voted in last week.

LENNY. I never voted for him.

CLAIRE. Yes, you did. By proxy. We were in Bermuda.

LENNY. I don't believe it. A goddam proxy new member spreads rumors about my best friend? Who does he play tennis with?

CLAIRE. He doesn't play tennis. He's a social member. He just eats lunches there.

LENNY. ... This son of a bitch is a non-playing proxy social new member who just eats lunches and spreads rumors? What does he do for a living?

CLAIRE. He sells BMW's

(*Charley's bedroom door opens and KEN steps out.*)

KEN. Did anyone else get here yet?

CLAIRE. Not to speak of, no.

LENNY. Is anything wrong?

KEN. (*Coming downstairs.*) Why? Does anything seem wrong to you?

LENNY. You mean aside from the fact there's no food, no guests, no host, no hostess, and that you and Chris only appear one-at-a-time and never together. Yes, I'd say something was wrong.

KEN. Okay. (*HE's looking at the floor, thinking.*) Okay, sit down, Len, Claire.

(*LENNY and CLAIRE sit. HE sits in the chair opposite.*)

KEN. All right, I can't keep this quiet anymore ... We've got a big problem on our hands.

LENNY. (*To Claire.*) Aha! What did I just say, Claire?

CLAIRE. You just said, "Aha!" What is it, Ken? Tell us.

KEN. Charley ... Charley, er ... Charley's been shot.

CLAIRE. *WHAT???*

LENNY. *SHOT???*

CLAIRE. Oh, my God!

LENNY. Jesus Christ!

CLAIRE. Don't tell me this!

LENNY. I can't catch my breath.

CLAIRE. Please don't let it be true.

LENNY. *(Wailing.) Charley, Charley, no! No, Charley, no!!!*

KEN. Take it easy, he's not dead. He's all right.

CLAIRE. He's not dead?

LENNY. He's all right?

KEN. He's alive. He's okay.

LENNY. Thank God, he's alive!

CLAIRE. Where was he shot?

KEN. In the head.

CLAIRE. In the *head?* The *head?* Oh, my, God, he was shot in the *head!!!*

KEN. It's all right. It's not bad. It's a superficial wound.

LENNY. Where did the bullet go?

KEN. Through his left ear lobe.

CLAIRE. The ear lobe? That's not too bad. I have holes in my ear lobes, it doesn't hurt.

LENNY. I saw this coming, I swear. The truth, Ken, did *she* do it?

KEN. Who?

LENNY. Myra, for crise sakes. Who else would it be?

KEN. Why would Myra shoot Charley?

CLAIRE. You don't know what's going on?

LENNY. You haven't heard?

KEN. No. What's going on?

CLAIRE. Charley's been having a hot affair with someone.

LENNY. It's not hot. You don't know if it's hot. Nobody said it was hot. (*To Ken.*) It's an affair. A plain affair.

KEN. (*To Lenny.*) Who told you this?

LENNY. Nobody told me *that*. What I heard was that *Myra* was having a thing.

KEN. A thing with who?

LENNY. A man. A guy. A fellow. A kid. Who knows?

CLAIRE. Someone else told me it was *Charley* who was having the affair.

KEN. What someone else?

LENNY. Some bitch at the club named Carole Newman.

CLAIRE. She is *not* a bitch. And she only told me what Harold Green told her.

KEN. Who's Harold Green?

LENNY. (*Quickly.*) Some goddamn proxy new social member who doesn't even play tennis. Comes to the club to eat lunches and spread rumors.

CLAIRE. Well, it seems to me Charley's the one who's having the affair if Myra was hysterical enough to shoot him.

KEN. Listen to me, will you, please? Myra didn't shoot him. *Charley* fired the gun. He tried to kill himself. It was attempted suicide.

CLAIRE. *SUICIDE???*

LENNY. Jesus Christ!

CLAIRE. Oh, my God!

LENNY. Don't tell me that.

CLAIRE. I don't believe it.

LENNY. (*Wailing.*) *No, Charley, no! Charley, Charley, no!*

KEN. Will you stop it! It's enough grieving. He's all right.

CLAIRE. Oh, Charley.

LENNY. It's all because of that no-good fucking Harold Green. That guy's out of the club. I can get the votes.

KEN. Can we stick to the main topic here? Nobody knows if anybody had an affair. I don't *know* why Charley shot himself.

LENNY. (*To Ken.*) So how is Myra taking this? My God, she must be a wreck.

CLAIRE. (*Rising.*) I should go up to her. Let me go up to her.

KEN. (*Stopping Claire.*) Don't go up to her. There's no point in going up to her. She's not here. She's gone.

CLAIRE. She's gone? Charley shoots himself in the head and Myra leaves the house?

LENNY. She walks out on him *now? Now* when he's laying up there with a bullet in his ear?

KEN. It's not in his ear. It went *through* his ear. WILL YOU LISTEN TO ME? PLEASE!!! ... Maybe she wasn't even here when it happened. Chris and I were driving up when we heard the shot. The front door was locked. I ran around the back and broke in the kitchen window.

CLAIRE. I saw that. I thought maybe Mai Li did it and maybe Myra fired her. But I didn't know then that Mai Li's mother was sick in Japan.

LENNY. (*To Claire.*) Don't talk for a while. Let me and Ken talk. You just listen. (*To Ken.*) So you broke in and rushed upstairs. Was he on the floor?

KEN. No. He was sitting in bed. The television was on. One of those evangelist shows. A bottle of Valium was on the night table. He was half-conscious. I figured maybe he took a couple of pills to make himself drowsy, put the gun to his head, started to fall asleep and shot himself through the ear.

CLAIRE. Is that blood on your shirt, Ken?

KEN. (*Looking down at his shirt.*) Where?

CLAIRE. Below the second stud.

KEN. Oh, shit, I didn't see that. That won't come out, will it?

LENNY. That's what you're worried about? A stain on your dress shirt?

KEN. I don't give a damn about my shirt. I'm trying to prevent Charley from getting a suicide rap. When the others walk in here, I don't want to explain to them how I got blood on my good silk shirt.

CLAIRE. You could borrow one of Charley's.

KEN. He's two sizes too big for me.

CLAIRE. I don't think they'd notice your cuffs if Charley has a big bandage on his ear and Myra's not even at the party.

LENNY. Let the man finish the story, will you, please? (*To Ken.*) Did he tell you anything? Did he say why he did it?

KEN. Not a word. He was barely conscious.

LENNY. Did he leave a note or anything?

KEN. He had a piece of paper in his hand. I tried to take it from him, but he tore it up and threw it into the john. He flushed before I could get to it.

CLAIRE. This is not happening. I'm not hearing this.

LENNY. *(To Ken.)* Did you call the police?

KEN. No. Just the doctor. We told him he fell down the stairs. As long as he wasn't hurt, I didn't want to make this thing public.

LENNY. We've *got* to call the police. This man is the Deputy Mayor of New York. We're talking front page on the *New York Times*. Pictures of Charley with his suit jacket over his head.

KEN. Exactly. That's what I'm trying to avoid till we find out what happened.

LENNY. If we keep this quiet, we're all accessories. I deal with the IRS boys. I'd be the first one they'd go after.

KEN. Why would they go after you?

LENNY. With attempted suicides, they open up everything. They'd want to see his books, his portfolio, his entire financial picture. They'd want to know how a Deputy Mayor could afford a big house like this.

KEN. That's no secret. Myra's a wealthy woman. She bought the house.

CHRIS. She did? I didn't know that.

LENNY. *(To Ken.)* You hear that? Now tomorrow it'll be all over the tennis club.

KEN. I'm not bringing in the police until I have to. I don't know what *you're* nervous about. Unless you have something to hide you don't want the IRS to know.

LENNY. Are you accusing me of hiding something? I'm the one who wants to bring in the police. Maybe *you're* the one who has something to hide. You make out his contracts. You made out his will.

KEN. Are you accusing me and Charley of conspiracy to defraud the city?

(*CAR LIGHTS flash on the window.*)

CLAIRE. I hear a car pulling up.

LENNY. (*To Ken, starting for the phone.*) If you're not calling the police, I am.

KEN. Oh, no you're not.

LENNY. You're telling me what I'm not going to do?

CLAIRE. (*At the window.*) It's pulling up the driveway.

LENNY. Suppose the neighbors heard the gunshot and have already called the police?

KEN. I'll deal with that problem when it arises.

LENNY. Maybe the car is the police. Then the problem has arosen.

CLAIRE. (*Looking out the window.*) It's a Volvo station wagon.

LENNY. A Volvo??!

KEN. Now I suppose you're worried it's the Swedish police.

CLAIRE. It's Ernie and Cookie.

LENNY. Ernie and Cookie?

KEN. (*To Claire.*) Why didn't you tell us?

CLAIRE. Why didn't you listen?

(*LENNY and KEN join Claire at the window. Charley's bedroom door opens and CHRIS steps out.*)

CHRIS. Ken, Myra and I are having trouble with her zipper.

KEN. No, you're not.

CHRIS. I'm not?

KEN. They know about it.

CHRIS. About Myra's zipper?

LENNY. We know that Myra's not here. Ken told us.

CHRIS. Oh.

CLAIRE. (*At the window.*) They're stopping to look at our BMW.

CHRIS. Did you tell them about Charley cutting his ear shaving?

KEN. They know *everything*. The gunshot, the ear lobe, the flushed note down the toilet, everything.

CHRIS. (*Angrily to Ken, coming downstairs.*) *Why didn't you tell me you told them?* ... They must think I'm an idiot.

LENNY. How is Charley?

CHRIS. He fell asleep. He's hugging the pillow with his thumb in this mouth.

CLAIRE. They're coming up to the house. I can't believe she's wearing a dress like that to a party like this.

KEN. All right, what do we do? Do we tell them or not?

CLAIRE. Why not? Ernie is Charley's analyst. Everything you tell your analyst remains confidential.

LENNY. What his *patients* tell him. We're not his patients. His patient is asleep sucking his thumb.

CHRIS. I can't believe I'm paying a baby sitter for this night.

(*The DOORBELL RINGS. THEY ALL freeze.*)

LENNY. So what did we decide? Do we call the police or not?

CHRIS. I say no. Cookie has her cooking show on television. Suppose she accidentally says something on the air?

LENNY. On a cooking show? Do you think she gives out suicide recipes?

KEN. I still think we say nothing till I find out what's happened. Better safe than sorry. Claire, open the door.

LENNY. Chris, get us some drinks. Let's look like we're having fun.

(*CHRIS rushes to the bar, gets drinks and sits beside Lenny on the sofa.*)

CLAIRE. So what is it? We're telling Ernie but we're not telling Cookie?

LENNY. *We're not telling either one of them!* I'm sorry we told you!

(*The DOORBELL RINGS.*)

LENNY. Just open the door!

KEN. Claire, don't open it until I get upstairs. If Charley wakes up, maybe I can get the story from him. (*Dashes upstairs to Charley's bedroom.*)

CHRIS. (*To Ken.*) I took the Valium away from him. I hid them in the medicine cabinet.

KEN. Gee, what a good hiding place. (*Exits into Charley's room.*)

(*CLAIRE crosses to the front door. LENNY and CHRIS quickly sit on the sofa with their drinks as if THEY're having an amusing chat.*)

LENNY. (*To Chris.*) So, Mrs. Thatcher replies, "I don't know, perhaps it's in my umbrella stand."

CLAIRE. (*At the front door.*) Are we ready?

LENNY. Yes! We're ready, we're ready!

(*CLAIRE smiles and opens the front door. CHRIS and LENNY break into loud LAUGHTER.*
ERNIE and COOKIE are at the door. ERNIE is in his early fifties, in a tux and carrying a gift box. COOKIE is in her forties, wears a god-awful evening gown. SHE carries a sausage-like cushion under her arm.)

CLAIRE. Cookie! Ernie! It's so good to see you. (*Hugs them both.*)

CHRIS. Oh, God, that is so funny, Lenny. You should have been an actor, I swear.

CLAIRE. Everybody, it's Ernie and Cookie.

LENNY. (*Still laughing.*) Hi, Ernie. Hi, Cookie.

CHRIS. (*Waves, laughing.*) Hi, Cookie. Hi, Ernie.

ERNIE. Hello, Chris. Hello, Lenny.

CHRIS. (*To Lenny.*) So go on with the story. What did Mr. Gorbachev say?

LENNY. (*After an awkward silence.*) Mr. Gorbachev? ... He said, "I don't know. I never ate cat food before."

(*There is much forced LAUGHTER.*)

ERNIE. Sorry we're late. Did we miss much?

CHRIS. You have *got* to get Lenny to tell you the story about Mrs. Thatcher and the cat food.

(*LENNY shoots Chris a dirty look.*)

ERNIE. (*Laughs.*) It sounds funny already. Heh heh heh.

COOKIE. Everyone looks so beautiful.

CLAIRE. Cookie, I am cr-azy about the dress. You always dig up the most original things. Where do you find them?

COOKIE. Oh, God, this is sixty years old. It was my grandmother's. She brought it from Russia.

CLAIRE. Didn't you wear that for Muscular Dystrophy in June?

COOKIE. No. Emphysema in August.

CLAIRE. (*Looking at the cushion.*) Oh, what a pretty cushion. Is that for Charley and Myra?

COOKIE. No, it's for my back. It went out again while I was dressing. (*SHE opens the pretzels, easily.*)

ERNIE. You all right, honey?

COOKIE. I'm fine, babe.

CHRIS. You and your back problems. It must be awful.

COOKIE. It's nothing. I can do everything but sit down and get up.

ERNIE. Hey, Lenny, is that your BMW? (*HE laughs.*) Looks like you put a lot of miles on in two days.

LENNY. A guy shoots out of a garage and blind-sides me. The car's got twelve miles on it. I've got a case of whiplash you wouldn't believe.

COOKIE. (*Crossing to other side of the room.*) Oh, I've had whiplash. Excruciating. My best friend had it for six years.

(*LENNY nods sardonically. SHE picks up the Steuben gift box.*)

COOKIE. Oh, this looks nice. Who brought this? (*SHE turns it to see the label but loses control and drops it.*) Oh, my God ... Did I break anything? (*SHE shakes the box. It RATTLES.*) What was it?

LENNY. Steuben glass.

COOKIE. Oh, don't tell me! Lenny! Claire! ... I'm so sorry.

ERNIE. It was an accident, honey. (*To Lenny and Claire.*) We'll replace it, of course.

LENNY. Sure, if you want. I don't care.

CHRIS. What about a drink, everyone?

ERNIE. I'll have something.

CHRIS. What do you want?

CLAIRE. I'll get it.

LENNY. (*Getting up.*) I'm right near the bar.

ERNIE. You're all going to get me a drink? Such friendly people. I'd love a bourbon, please.

(*CHRIS crosses to the bar.*)

COOKIE. I should have let what's-her-name pick it up. Moo Loo.

CHRIS. Mai Li ... Here you go, Ern. (*Gives Ernie his drink.*)

COOKIE. Where's Ken?

CLAIRE. Ken? Ken's with Charley.

COOKIE. And Myra?

CLAIRE. Myra's with Ken ... They're waiting for Myra to get dressed.

COOKIE. (*Grabbing the back of a chair and screaming.*) Ooooh! Ooooh! Ooooh!

CLAIRE. What is it?

COOKIE. A spasm. It's gone. It's all right. It just shoots up my back and goes.

ERNIE. You all right, poops?

COOKIE. I'm fine, puppy.

LENNY. Listen, maybe we should all sit outside. It's such a beautiful evening.

ERNIE. (*Smiles.*) Okay. Okay, you kids, what's going on here?

CLAIRE. What do you mean?

ERNIE. You think I don't notice everyone's acting funny? Three people want to get me drinks. Chris wants me to hear this funny story. Lenny wants to get us all outside. Everyone creating a diversion. Why? I don't know. Am I right?

CHRIS. No wonder you're such a high-priced doctor. OK ... Someone's going to have to tell them.

LENNY. Tell them what?

CHRIS. About the surprise.

LENNY. What surprise?

CHRIS. The surprise about the party.

COOKIE. What surprise about the party?

CHRIS. Well, I think it's the cutest thing, isn't it, Claire?

CLAIRE. Oh, God, yes.

CHRIS. Tell them about it.

CLAIRE. No, you tell it better than I do.

COOKIE. I'm sorry. I think I'm going to have to sit down.

CHRIS. I'll help you.

LENNY. I'll do it.

CLAIRE. I've got her.

(*THEY all help lower Cookie onto the sofa, beside Ernie.*)

COOKIE. The cushion. I need the cushion.

LENNY. Here it is. (*HE puts the cushion behind her back.*)

ERNIE. You all right, chicken?

COOKIE. I'm fine, Pops ... So what's the big surprise about?

CHRIS. Well ... Charley and Myra decided ... because they were going to have their closest friends over to celebrate their tenth anniversary ... they weren't going to have any ... servants.

COOKIE. (*Nods.*) Uh huh.

CHRIS. No Mai Li, no anybody.

COOKIE. (*Nods.*) Uh huh.

CHRIS. Isn't that terrific. No help. Just us.

COOKIE. Why is that terrific?

CHRIS. Because!! We're all going to pitch in. Like in the old days. Before money. Before success. Like when we were all just starting out. Those were the best times in our lives, don't you think?

COOKIE. No, I hated those times. I love success.

CHRIS. But don't you find these are greedier times. Lazier, more selfish. Nobody wants to work anymore.

COOKIE. I work fourteen hours a day. I cook thirty-seven meals a week. I cook on my television show. I cook for my family. I cook for my neighbors. I cook for my dogs. I was looking forward to a relaxed evening. (*SHE reconsiders.*) But I don't want to spoil the fun. What do we have to do?

CLAIRE. We have to cook.

COOKIE. You mean all of us cooking in the kitchen together?

CHRIS. Everyone except Charley and Myra. Claire and I told them to stay up there and relax. We'll call them when we're ready.

COOKIE. What are we going to make?

CLAIRE. It's all laid out. Roast ham, smoked turkey, duck and pasta?

ERNIE. Roast ham? Duck? ... That's too much cholesterol for me.

LENNY. Ernie, we didn't come here to live longer. Just to have a good time.

COOKIE. I just don't understand why we're all wearing our best clothes to cook a dinner.

CLAIRE. That's not your best clothes. It's a fifty-year-old Polish dress.

COOKIE. A sixty-year-old Russian dress.

ERNIE. The dress is hardly an issue worth arguing about.

COOKIE. I didn't say we wouldn't cook it.

ERNIE. She didn't say we wouldn't cook it. Why is everyone getting so worked up about this?

CLAIRE. All right, Ernie, let's not turn this into group therapy, please.

ERNIE. This is nothing like group therapy, Claire. You, of all people, should know that.

LENNY. Oh, terrific. Let's just name all the people in your Thursday night group, Ernie, heh?

COOKIE. Why are Ernie and I being attacked? We just walked in the door.

CHRIS. Please lower your voices. We're going to spoil the surprise for Charley and Myra.

ERNIE. What surprise? It was their idea.

COOKIE. Listen, I don't want to take the blame for ruining this party. (*To the Group.*) I'll do all the cooking myself and Ernie'll do the serving.

ERNIE. Honey, no one's asking you to do that.

CHRIS & CLAIRE. If she wants to do it, let her. Sure. Why not? Fine with us.

LEN. If it makes her happy, she can clean up, too.

COOKIE. (*Struggling to her feet.*) Okay, then it's settled. Just give me forty-five minutes. I promise you this is going to be the best dinner party we ever had.

(*Suddenly, we hear a GUNSHOT from Charley's room.*)

COOKIE. Oh, my God!

(*EVERYONE freezes. COOKIE falls back onto the sofa.*)

CLAIRE. Oh, give me a break.

ERNIE. What the hell was that?

(*Charley's bedroom door opens and KEN, looking harassed, comes out, looks over the railing and tries to appear calm.*)

KEN. It's fine. It's okay. It's all under control. Hi, Ernie. Hi, Cookie ... Oh, Chris, honey, could I see you up here for a minute ... (*HE smiles at them and returns to Charley's bedroom.*)

CHRIS. (*Politely.*) Would you all excuse me for a minute? I hate when this happens. (*SHE goes calmly up the stairs and into Charley's room.*)

ERNIE. Am I crazy or was that a gunshot?

LENNY. A gunshot? Nooo. I think it was a car backfiring.

ERNIE. In Charley's bedroom?

COOKIE. Ernie, maybe you should go up and see.

LENNY. Why? Chris and Ken and Charley and Myra are up there. There's more of them than us.

COOKIE. You just can't ignore a gunshot. Ernie, please go up and see.

LENNY. Oh, I know. I know. I know exactly what it was ... It was a balloon. They've been blowing up party balloons up there all day.

ERNIE. What kind of a balloon was that, the Goodyear blimp? ... I'm going up.

LENNY. Then how are we going to get the dinner ready? Charley and Myra must be starved. You and Cookie get started. I'll have a white wine spritzer, Ern. Claire, why don't you put on some music? (*Rushing upstairs.*) I'll be right down. Let me know if Dr. Doolittle calls. (*H E disappears into Charley's bedroom. The TELEPHONE rings.*)

CLAIRE. I'll get it. (*SHE crosses to the phone.*)

ERNIE. I still think it sounded like a gunshot.

COOKIE. Let's get dinner started, Ern. Help me up. (*Tries to get up out of the sofa.*)

CLAIRE. (*Into the phone.*) Hello? ... Who? Dr. Cusack? Yes, he is. Who is it, please?

ERNIE. (*To Claire.*) Is that for me?

CLAIRE. (*Into phone.*) Uh huh. Uh huh. (*To Ernie.*) It's a conference call. Mr. and Mrs. Klein, Mr. and Mrs. Platt, Mr. and Mrs. Fishman.

ERNIE. Oh, it's my Friday night group. I have a telephone session with them.

COOKIE. Go on, honey. I can get up myself.

(*ERNIE runs into the kitchen.*)

CLAIRE. (*Into phone.*) He's coming, folks. (*The other line on PHONE RINGS. SHE switches buttons.*) Hello? ... Yes it is. No, my husband, just called.

(*COOKIE gets down on the floor and crawls on her hands and knees.*)

CLAIRE. Yes, I'll tell him. (*SHE holds the phone.*)

LENNY. (*Comes out of Charley's room.*) Who's on the phone?

CLAIRE. Dr. Dudley's service.

LENNY. (*Nods and comes downstairs. HE sees Cookie crawling on the floor.*) Oh, my God. What's that?

CLAIRE. It's Cookie.

COOKIE. It's all right. I do this all the time. It takes the pressure off my back.

LENNY. Where's Ernie?

CLAIRE. (*Pointing toward the kitchen.*) In there. He's got a session with his Friday night group.

LENNY. They're all in the kitchen?

CLAIRE. No. On the telephone.

COOKIE. (*Crawling toward the dining room.*) Ah! Ah! Ah!

LENNY. Your back again?

COOKIE. No. Little shirt pins on the floor. (*SHE crawls off into the kitchen.*) Ah! Ah! Ah!

LENNY. (*To Claire.*) She must be such fun to live with.

CLAIRE. What happened upstairs? Is Charley all right?

LENNY. He was sleeping. Ken wanted to hide the gun in the closet so Charley wouldn't find it. He tripped on

Charley's slippers and the gun went off next to his head. He can't hear a thing in both ears.

CLAIRE. Ken or Charley?

LENNY. Ken. Charley was out cold from the Valium. (*Sees the phone is hung up.*)

CLAIRE. They hung up. I already took the message.

LENNY. You couldn't tell me that while I was on the balcony? What'd they say?

CLAIRE. They said Dr. Dudley already called this number. He doesn't want to be called out of the theatre again.

LENNY. (*Angrily re-dials the phone.*) I'm getting a new doctor. I'm not putting my life in the hands of the drama critic for Mount Sinai Hospital. (*Into phone.*) Hello? This is Leonard Ganz again. Dr. Dudley did *not* call this number. Please have him call me back. It's important. (*HE hangs up the phone.*)

CLAIRE. So what did Ken want Chris upstairs for?

LENNY. To call Ken's doctor to ask him what to do for his ears. He wouldn't be able to hear what the doctor was saying on the phone. I've got to get back upstairs. (*HE starts back upstairs.*)

CLAIRE. You mean she told the doctor a gun went off? Then she'll have to explain about Charley.

LENNY. No. She was going to say Ken was outside and a manhole cover blew up next to him.

CLAIRE. That's a good idea.

LENNY. Except the doctor wasn't in. His service said he was still at the theatre. There must be some kind of flu going around on Broadway. (*HE runs upstairs. When HE hits the top step, the PHONE rings.*) They purposely wait till I get on top of the stairs. Answer that, will you?

CLAIRE. (*Crossing to the phone.*) This is all too hard to follow. I need a bookmark in my head or something. (*SHE picks up the phone.*) Hello? Oh, Dr. Dudley, thanks for calling back. (*To Lenny.*) You want to speak to him?

LENNY. (*Running down the stairs.*) No. I'm taking a stress test.

CLAIRE. You know, if Ernie can't figure out something's wrong here, I'm not going to his group anymore.

LENNY. (*Picking up the phone.*) Hello, Dr. Dudley? ... Thanks for calling back ... Well, some idiot nailed me in my BMW about twenty minutes ago. I've got a little whiplash here ... Charley? Charley Brock? ... No, I wasn't calling about Charley. Why? (*Covering the phone, to Claire.*) Jesus! Dr. Dudley is Charley's doctor, too. (*Into the phone.*) No, Charley's a lot better. He's resting now ... Chris Gorman? You know Ken and Chris? Yes, I think she did call. (*Covering the phone, to Claire.*) He's Ken's doctor, too.

CLAIRE. Maybe he has a franchise.

LENNY. Will you make yourself busy. Put on some music. (*Into phone.*) Dr. Dudley? I'm sorry. A cold compress? ... Good idea. Let me connect you to Chris. Hold on. (*HE presses "Hold" button, then looks at extension numbers.*) Which button rings in Charley's room?

CLAIRE. Why? Who's going to hear it up there?

LENNY. (*Not covering phone.*) Jesus, you are a pain in the ass. I'd better run up and get Chris. (*Taking the phone off "Hold".*) Dr. Dudley? ... What? ... Oh, yes, my wife has a pain, too. It's no bother. Can you hold for Chirs, please? (*Putting the phone on "Hold," then dashing upstairs.*) We owe this guy a gift. Let's give him Cookie as a patient. See where Ernie is with my drink, will you? (*HE goes into Charley's bedroom.*)

(*The dining room door opens and ERNIE comes out with a drink.*)

ERNIE. I thought I heard Lenny in here. I have his spritzer.

CLAIRE. I'll hold it for him. How's Cookie? (*SHE takes the drink.*)

ERNIE. Not well. I gave her some aspirins for her back, but she dropped them in the sauce.

CLAIRE. Good. Then we'll all get rid of *our* headaches.

ERNIE. Did Lenny say what that sound was?

CLAIRE. The gunshot?

ERNIE. It *was* a gunshot?

CLAIRE. No, I was referring to the sound you *thought* was a gunshot.

ERNIE. It wasn't a balloon, I know that.

CLAIRE. No. It was a can of shaving cream. It exploded.

ERNIE. Shaving cream exploded?

CLAIRE. It's all right. It washes off.

ERNIE. Incredible.

COOKIE. (*Sticking her head out the dining room door.*) Ernie? I need you to put out some garbage.

ERNIE. I'm not through talking to my group yet.

COOKIE. They're fighting with each other. I put them on hold.

(*COOKIE and ERNIE exit into the kitchen.*

Charley's bedroom door opens and LENNY and KEN come out. KEN holds a towel over his ears.)

LENNY. It'll clear up in a minute. These things don't last long.

KEN. You think this'll last long?

LENNY. *(Opening the guest room door.)* Lie down in the guest room for a while, Ken. You'll feel better.

KEN. *(Looking into the guest room.)* Maybe if I lie down in the guest room for a while ...

LENNY. Right.

CLAIRE. *(To Lenny.)* What did the doctor say to Chris?

LENNY. He referred her to another doctor. He's not feeling well himself ... My neck is killing me again. Where's my spritzer?

KEN. *(Coming out of the guest room; to Lenny.)* Is your sister here?

LENNY. No, my *spritzer!!* Come on, Ken. I'll heat that towel up again.

KEN. Don't tell your sister about Charley. Not till we hear the whole story.

(THEY go into the guest room.
The kitchen door opens and COOKIE comes out. SHE holds a ladle in one hand and her other hand supports a bag of ice on her hip.)

COOKIE. I've got a problem, Claire, can you help me? Ernie went out the kitchen door to put out some garbage bags and the door locked. My hands are full of grease. Could you let him back in?

CLAIRE. Of course. We would all miss him terribly. (*SHE exits to the kitchen.*)

ERNIE. (*Enters through the front door on his own.*) I purposely went around so you wouldn't have to go to the door.

(*Charley's bedroom door opens and CHRIS steps out.*)

CHRIS. Oh, hi! ... Where's Claire?

COOKIE. She went out to the kitchen to let Ernie in.

CHRIS. (*Looking at Ernie.*) Oh. Okay (*SHE smiles and goes back into Charley's bedroom, closing the door.*)

(*The dining room door opens and CLAIRE comes out.*)

CLAIRE. Oh, there you are ... Cookie, the water's boiling over on the pasta.

COOKIE. Why didn't you turn it down?

CLAIRE. I don't know. I don't watch your show.

COOKIE. I'll get it. Ernie, get another bag of ice. I'm melting. (*SHE exits into the kitchen.*)

ERNIE. (*Following Cookie, to Claire.*) I'm beginning to feel like one of my patients. (*HE laughs and goes to the kitchen.*)

(*Charley's door opens and CHRIS comes out.*)

CHRIS. (*Big smile.*) Well, everything is just fine.

CLAIRE. It's all right. They're in the kitchen.

CHRIS. God, I'd smoke a Havana cigar if I had one. (*Coming downstairs, scratching under her arms.*) I'm getting hives under my arms. (*Going to bar to make herself a vodka.*) Did you hear about Ken? He's deaf.

CLAIRE. He's better off. He's out of this thing now.

CHRIS. Why are we protecting Charley this way? Ken is deaf, Lenny can't turn his neck, Cookie's walking like a giraffe, I'm getting a blood condition. (*SHE scratches.*) For what? One more gunshot, the whole world will know anyway.

CLAIRE. The whole world isn't interested. Paraguay and Bolivia don't give a rat's ass.

(*We hear another CAR coming up the driveway.*)

LENNY. (*Coming out of the guest room.*) There's another car coming up.

(*We see the HEADLIGHTS flash on the window.*)

LENNY. Was anyone else invited?

CHRIS. Harry and Joan, but they cancelled. They went to Venezuela. But they said they'd call tonight.

LENNY. From Venezuela?

CLAIRE. Jeez, maybe they *will* hear about it in Bolivia.

LENNY. So who's coming up the driveway?

CHRIS. Maybe it's Myra. Maybe she's come back.

LENNY. Myra drives a Porsche. This is an Audi. (*HE comes halfway down the stairs.*)

CLAIRE. Ask Ken. He might know.

LENNY. Ken is reading lips right now. I don't think he can pick up on "Audi."

(*We hear a loud CRASH from the kitchen.*)

LENNY. Jesus, what the hell was that?

CHRIS. Cookie just blew up the micro-wave, what else?

LENNY. Chris, go inside and see what happened. Claire, go to the window and see who's coming. I'll go up and see how Ken and Charley are doing ... (*HE has been gesturing with a white towel.*) I feel like I'm at the fucking Alamo. (*HE rushes upstairs, just as:*)

(*The dining room door flies open and ERNIE comes out, flicking his fingers in pain.*)

ERNIE. Damn, I burned my fingers! Hot hot hot, oh, *God*, It's hot!

CHRIS. Oh, dear.

ERNIE. Sonofagun, that hurts. Oh, fuckerini!

CLAIRE. What happened?

ERNIE. (*Quickly.*) Cookie dropped her ice bag and slipped against the stove. The hot platter was about to fall on her, so I lifted it up. Then I dropped it on the table and it broke the water pitcher and the glass shattered on her arm and she's bleeding like hell. I got a dish towel on her wrist and I propped her up against a cabinet. But I need some bandages for her arm and some ointment for my fingers. I never saw anything happen so fast.

LENNY. I can't believe he's in pain and said all that without missing a word.

CLAIRE. (*To Lenny.*) Get the bandages. Why are you standing there?

LENNY. I was hoping there was more to the story. (*HE rushes into Charley's room and closes the door.*)

ERNIE. I'm sorry, Claire. Did you ask for a drink?

CLAIRE. Listen, you have other things to think about.

ERNIE. Right. (*HE exits.*)

(*CHRIS and CLAIRE stare at each other.*)

CLAIRE. You know what this night is beginning to remind me of? ... *Platoon.*

(*A car DOOR slams outside.*)

CHRIS. There's the car. I don't even want to know who it is. Why don't you go and look?
CLAIRE. Like it's going to be good news, right? (*SHE crosses to the window and looks out.*) It's Glenn and Cassie.
CHRIS. Glenn and Cassie Cooper? Together?
CLAIRE. That's how they're walking.
CHRIS. I heard they were having trouble.
CLAIRE. Not walking. (*SHE comes away from the window.*)
CHRIS. Jesus! Do you know that Glenn is running for the State Senate in Poughkeepsie.
CLAIRE. So?
CHRIS. That's all he needs is to walk in here and be part of a hushed-up suicide attempt. He can kiss his career goodbye.
CLAIRE. Maybe Ken'll figure this all out before they ring the doorbell.

(*The DOORBELL rings.*)

CLAIRE. Well, it's going to be a tough campaign.

CHRIS. Listen, I have to go to the bathroom. You get the door, I'll be right out. (*SHE starts for the powder room.*)

CLAIRE. Wait a minute! I haven't gone since I got here.

CHRIS. Yes you did. In Mai Li's room

CLAIRE. Yes, but no one was at the door then.

CHRIS. The hell with it. Someone else'll get the door. Come on.

(*THEY BOTH go into the powder room and close the door behind them.*
The DOORBELL rings again. LENNY comes out of the guest room.)

LENNY. Isn't anybody going to get the door? ... Chris? ... Claire? ...

KEN. (*Peering out from the guest room.*) Are you talking to me?

LENNY. No, Ken. Put the towels back on your ears. (*Yelling down.*) Claire? ... Chris? ... Where are you? ... Ah, screw it. I'm beginning to feel like my car. (*HE goes back into the guest room and closes the door.*)

(*The dining room door opens and ERNIE comes out with paper towels wrapped around the fingers on both hands. HE is wearing an apron. HE shouts up.*)

ERNIE. Lenny? You got those bandages?

(*The DOORBELL rings again.*)

ERNIE. Nobody getting that door? ... These kids are up to something, I know it. (*HE crosses to the front door and tries to open it with burned fingers. HE is finally successful.*)

(*GLENN and CASSIE COOPER, a handsome couple, stand there in evening clothes. GLENN holds a gift from Ralph Lauren's. THEY seem very much on edge with each other.*)

ERNIE. (*Smiles.*) Hello.
GLENN. Good evening.

(*THEY walk in, look around. ERNIE closes the door with his foot.*)

ERNIE. Good evening. I don't know where everyone is.
CASSIE. You mean we're the first?
ERNIE. No. Everyone's here. They're just – spread out a little.
GLENN. Could I have a drink, please? Double Scotch, straight up.
CASSIE. (*Not looking at Ernie.*) Perrier with lime, no ice.
ERNIE. Sure. Fine. I don't believe we've met. I'm Ernie Cusack.
GLENN. (*Coolly, nods.*) Hello, Ernie.
ERNIE. Excuse my hands. Little accident in the kitchen.
GLENN. Sorry to hear it.
ERNIE. I would stay and chat but my wife is bleeding in the kitchen.

GLENN. Your wife?

ERNIE. Cookie. A water pitcher broke, cut her arm. I burned my fingers.

GLENN. That's a shame.

ERNIE. Nothing to worry about. We'll have dinner ready soon. Nice meeting you both. (*HE returns to the kitchen.*)

GLENN. I wonder why they're not using the Chinese girl?

CASSIE. Do I look all right?

GLENN. Yes. Fine.

CASSIE. I feel so frumpy.

GLENN. God, no. You look beautiful.

CASSIE. My hair isn't right, is it? I saw you looking at it in the car.

GLENN. No, I wasn't.

CASSIE. What were you looking at then?

GLENN. The road, I suppose.

CASSIE. I can always tell when you hate what I'm wearing.

GLENN. I love that dress. I always have.

CASSIE. This is the first time I've worn it.

GLENN. I always have admired your taste is what I meant.

CASSIE. It's so hard to please you sometimes.

GLENN. What did I say?

CASSIE. It's what you *don't* say that really drives me crazy.

GLENN. What I *don't* say? ... How can it drive you crazy if I don't say it?

CASSIE. I don't know. It's the looks that you give me.

GLENN. I wasn't giving you any looks.

CASSIE. You look at me all the time.

GLENN. Because you're always asking me to look at you.

CASSIE. It would be nice if I didn't have to ask you, wouldn't it?

GLENN. It would be nice if you didn't need me to look, which would make it unnecessary to ask.

CASSIE. I can't ever get any support from you. You've got all the time in the world for everything and everyone else, but I've got to draw blood to get your attention when I walk in a room.

GLENN. We walked in the room together. It was already done. Cassie, please don't start. We're forty-five minutes late as it is. I don't want to ruin this night for Charley and Myra.

CASSIE. We're forty-five minutes late because you scowled at every dress I tried on.

GLENN. I didn't scowl, I smiled. You always think my smile looks like a scowl. You think my grin looks like a frown, and my frown looks like a yawn.

CASSIE. Don't sneer at me.

GLENN. It wasn't a sneer. It was a peeve.

CASSIE. God, this conversation is so banal. I can't believe any of the things I'm saying. We sound like some fucking TV couple.

GLENN. Oh, now we're going to get into language, right?

CASSIE. No, Mr. Perfect. I will not get into any language. I don't want to risk a scowl, a frown, a yawn, a peeve or a sneer. God forbid I should show a human imperfection, I'd wake up with the divorce papers in my hand.

GLENN. What is this thing lately with divorce? Where does that come from? I don't look at you sometimes because I'm afraid you're thinking you don't like the way I'm looking at you.

CASSIE. I don't know what the hell you want from me, Glenn. I really don't.

GLENN. I don't want *any*thing from you. I mean I would like it to be the way we were before we got to be the way we are.

CASSIE. God, you suffocate me sometimes ... I want to go home.

GLENN. Go home? We just got here. We haven't even seen anyone yet.

CASSIE. I don't know how I'm going to get through this night. They all know what's going on. They're your friends. Jesus, and you expect me to behave like nothing's happening.

GLENN. Nothing is happening. What are you talking about?

CASSIE. Don't you fucking lie to me. The whole goddam city knows about you and that cheap little chippy bimbo.

GLENN. Will you keep it down? Nothing is going on. You're blowing this up out of all proportions. I hardly know the woman. She's on the Democratic Fund Raising Committee. I met her and her husband at two cocktail parties, for God sakes.

CASSIE. Two cocktail parties, heh?

GLENN. Yes! Two cocktail parties.

CASSIE. You think I'm stupid?

GLENN. No.

CASSIE. You think I'm blind?

GLENN. No.

CASSIE. You think I don't know what's been going on?

GLENN. Yes, because you don't.

CASSIE. I'm going to tell you something, Glenn. Are you listening?

GLENN. Don't you see my ears perking up?

CASSIE. I've known about you and Carole Newman for a year now.

GLENN. Amazing, since I only met her four months ago. Now I'm asking you to please lower your voice. That butler must be listening to everything.

CASSIE. You think I care about a butler and a bleeding cook? My friends know about your bimbo, what do I care about domestic help?

GLENN. I don't know what's gotten into you, Cassie. Do my political ambitions bother you? Are you threatened somehow because I'm running for the Senate?

CASSIE. *State* Senate! *State* Senate! Don't make it sound like we're going to Washington. We're going to Albany. Twenty-three degrees below zero in the middle of winter Albany. You're not *Time*'s Man of the Year yet, you understand, honey?

GLENN. (*Turning away.*) Oh, boy, oh, boy, oh boy!

CASSIE. What was that?

GLENN. (*Deliberately.*) Oh-boy, oh-boy, oh-boy!

CASSIE. Oh, like I'm behaving badly, right? I'm the shrew witch wife who's giving you such a hard time. I'll tell you something, Mr. *State* Senator. I'm not the only one who knows what's going on. People are talking, kiddo. Trust me.

GLENN. What do you mean? You haven't said anything to anyone, have you?

CASSIE. Oh, is that what you're worried about? Your reputation? Your career? Your place in American history? You know what your place in American history will be? ... A commemorative stamp of you and the bimbo in a motel together.

GLENN. You are so hyper tonight, Cassie. You're out of control. You've been rubbing your quartz crystal again, haven't you? I told you to throw those damn crystals away. They're dangerous. They're like petrified cocaine.

(*CASSIE is looking through her purse.*)

GLENN. ... Don't take it out, Cassie. Don't rub your crystal at the party. It makes you crazy.

(*SHE takes out her crystal. HE grabs for it.*)

GLENN. Put it away. Don't let my friends see what you're doing.

CASSIE. Fine. Don't let *my* friends see what *you're* doing.

(*The guest room door opens. LENNY comes out onto the balcony.*)

LENNY. Glenn! Cassie! I thought it was you. How you doing?

KEN. (*From inside the guest room.*) I'm feeling better, thanks.

LENNY. Not you, Ken. It's Glenn and Cassie.

GLENN. (*Big smile.*) We're fine. Just great. Hi, Len ... Cassie, it's Len ... Cassie.

CASSIE. (*A quick nod.*) Leonard.

LENNY. Did it suddenly freeze up out there?

GLENN. Freeze up?

LENNY. Isn't that an icicle Cassie has there?

GLENN. No. It's a quartz crystal.

LENNY. Oh. Where's Chris and Claire?

KEN. (*From the guest room.*) Did somebody come in?

LENNY. (*Angrily, to Ken.*) GLENN AND CASSIE!! I *TOLD* YOU!! (*To Glenn.*) It's Ken. His ears are stuffed up. Bad cold ... Who let you in?

GLENN. The butler.

LENNY. The butler? The butler's here?

GLENN. He's getting us drinks.

LENNY. Is he alone?

GLENN. No, the cook's with him.

LENNY. Mai Li? God, what a relief. They came back. We didn't have any help here for a while.

GLENN. Really? Where's Charley and Myra?

LENNY. Charley and Myra? I guess they're in their room.

KEN. (*From the guest room.*) My towel fell off, Lenny.

LENNY. (*Angrily, to Ken.*) I'LL GET YOU A TOWEL. I'VE GOT TO GET THE BANDAGES FIRST. (*To Glenn.*) Excuse me, kids. I've got to get some bandages. (*HE knocks on Charley's door.*) Charley? Myra? Is it all right if I come in? (*In Myra's voice.*) Sure, come on in. (*HE goes into Charley's room and closes the door.*)

(*The guest room door opens and KEN comes out.*)

KEN. Lenny? ... Lenny, where'd you go?

(*GLENN and CASSIE look up.*)

GLENN. Ken? Hi. It's Glenn and Cassie.

KEN. Lenny? Is that you? (*HE looks down.*) Who's that? Glenn? Is that Glenn?

GLENN. Yes. And Cassie. I hear you have a cold.

KEN. You think I look old? I haven't been sleeping well lately ... Hi, Cassie. Do the others know you're here?

GLENN. Yes. We just saw Lenny.

KEN. Have you seen Lenny?

GLENN. Yes. He went into Charley's room.

KEN. I'm sorry. I can't hear anything. A manhole cover just blew up next to my ear.

GLENN. That's terrible.

KEN. I said, "A manhole cover just blew up next to my ear."

GLENN. Yes. I hear you.

KEN. I'm sorry. I can't hear you. Anyone getting you a drink?

GLENN. Yes, the butler.

KEN. Sorry, there's no help here. They're in the Orient somewhere.

CASSIE. (*To Glenn.*) I think he's gone dotty.

KEN. Yes, a hot toddy would be nice. I'm going to see if Lenny's in Charley's room. We're all coming down soon. (*HE knocks on Charley's door.*) Myra? Mind if I come in?

LENNY. (*As Myra, from inside.*) Sure, honey. Come on in.

(*KEN goes into Charley's room.*)

CASSIE. I'll be right back.

GLENN. Where are you going?

CASSIE. To rinse off my crystal. (*Starting to the powder room.*) ... I suppose you'd like to make a *quick* phone call while I'm gone, heh? (*SHE tries to open the powder room door, but it's locked.*) Anyone in there?

CHRIS. (*From inside.*) Who is it?

CASSIE. Cassie. Who's that?

CHRIS. (*From inside.*) It's Chris ... Just a minute, Cass. (*We hear a FLUSH. CHRIS comes out and closes the door.*) I didn't hear you ring, Cassie. I would have opened the door. Hi, Glenn. (*SHE crosses to him and gives him a kiss. By now she's getting pretty crocked from her vodkas.*)

GLENN. Hi. Listen, is anything going on here?

CHRIS. I don't know ... Who have you seen?

GLENN. Well, Lenny and Ken for just a second. And the butler and Mai Li.

CHRIS. You saw Mai Li and the butler? My God, I must have been in there for a long time.

CASSIE. Are you through in the bathroom?

CHRIS. Me? Yes. Sure.

CASSIE. (*Tries the door again, but it's locked.*) You left it locked.

CLAIRE. (*From inside.*) Who is it?

CASSIE. Cassie. Who's that?

CLAIRE. (*From inside.*) It's Claire. Just a minute, Cass. (*We hear a FLUSH. The door opens and CLAIRE comes out.*) Hi, Cass. Hi, Glenn. Don't you look beautiful ... Where are the boys?

GLENN. Well, Lenny and Ken are up with Charley and Myra. Myra sounded very excited.

CLAIRE. You spoke to Myra?

GLENN. No. I heard her talk to Ken and Len.

CLAIRE. I'd love to have a copy of that conversation.

CASSIE. Is anyone else in the bathroom, because I have to go. (*SHE looks inside, then goes in and locks the door behind her.*)

CHRIS. (*To Claire.*) Mai Li and the butler are here.

CLAIRE. You're kidding. Where's Ernie and Cookie.

GLENN. I just met Ernie. Isn't he the butler?

CHRIS. Oh. No. Okay. We've got that one cleared up.

GLENN. Then they're just back from the Orient?

CHRIS. I imagine so. You're so well informed.

GLENN. Why is everyone up in Charley's room?

CHRIS. Oh. There was something on TV they all wanted to watch.

CLAIRE. Right. Very good, Chris.

(*Charley's bedroom door opens, and LENNY comes out.*)

LENNY. (*Jovial.*) Well, this is beginning to look like a party.

GLENN. What were you all watching up there?

LENNY. Up where?

GLENN. On TV.

CHRIS. (*To Lenny.*) The thing you went up to watch with Ken and Charley and Myra.

LENNY. Oh. OH! That thing. That show. The PBS Special on what's-his-name?

CLAIRE. ... Hitler?

LENNY. Yes. The thing on Hitler. (*HE comes downstairs, glaring at Claire.*)

GLENN. On their tenth anniversary you wanted to watch a special on Hitler?

LENNY. Hitler as a boy. A whole new slant on him.

ERNIE. (*Comes out of the dining room door. HE carries two drinks.*) Dinner's coming along. (*To Glenn.*) Double Scotch, straight up.

GLENN. Oh, thanks.

ERNIE. Lenny, have you got the bandages?

LENNY. The bandages? Yes. I have them. I left them on Hitler ... On the television. I'll be right back. (*HE runs back upstairs and into Charley's room, closing the door behind him.*)

GLENN. Listen, I'm sorry. I mistook you for the butler.

ERNIE. I kind of thought you did. No, I'm an analyst.

GLENN. Oh, for pete sakes. I'm Glenn ... How's your wife doing?

ERNIE. The spaghetti's boiling, but the duck is still frozen.

GLENN. No, I meant her arm.

ERNIE. Oh, not too bad. She's a trouper. Her fingers are cramping up a little.

GLENN. Maybe she ought to see a doctor. Charley has one ten minutes from here, Dr. Dudley.

CHRIS. Oh. We called him. He's busy.

ERNIE. You called about Cookie's arm?

CLAIRE. No, about Lenny's neck.

GLENN. Lenny's neck?

CHRIS. And when the doctor called back, we told him about Ken's ears.

ERNIE. (*To Glenn.*) Isn't that incredible? From a can of shaving cream exploding?

GLENN. I thought it was a manhole cover.

CLAIRE. It was. But the pressure from the manhole cover made the shaving cream can explode.

ERNIE. (*To Glenn.*) I didn't hear that.

LENNY. (*Coming out of Charley's room with the bandages. HE runs downstairs.*) I got 'em. I got 'em.

GLENN. There certainly is some excitement around here.

CLAIRE. (*To Lenny.*) Guess who Glenn's doctor is?

LENNY. You're kidding. I wish I did his taxes.

ERNIE. Wait a minute! Glenn Cooper! From Poughkeepsie. You're running for the State Senate.

GLENN. That's right.

ERNIE. I have a good friend who knows you very well.

GLENN. Really? Who's that?

ERNIE. Harold Green.

LENNY. Harold Green! (*LENNY drops the bandages.*)

CLAIRE. Harold Green?

GLENN. Sure. I know Harold Green. We went to the University of Pennsylvania together. I haven't seen him in years.What's he doing now?

LENNY. He's a proxy new social member who just eats lunches and doesn't play tennis.

GLENN. Oh. At your club? (*GLENN hands the bandages to Ernie.*)

LENNY. Ernie, Cookie's waiting in the emergency room

ERNIE. Right. (*To Glenn.*) There's your wife's Perrier. Nice to meet you, Glenn. (*As HE exits to the kitchen.*) ... thought I was the butler.

(*Charley's door opens and KEN comes out.*)

KEN. Somebody! Please! I need a drink real bad.

GLENN. How's your ears, Ken?

KEN. (*Coming downstairs.*) A beer would be fine, thanks.

GLENN. Maybe Charley has some ear drops. (*To Lenny.*) Did you see any in the medicine cabinet when you were getting the bandages?

LENNY. No, I didn't think of that.

GLENN. I'll go up and look.

(*HE starts to go up the stairs. LENNY and KEN block him.*)

LENNY. No. I remember. I looked. There weren't any. I forgot I looked.

(*The TELEPHONE rings.*)

KEN. Is there a cat in here?

CHRIS. A cat?

KEN. I just heard a cat meow. (*The TELEPHONE rings again.*) There it is again.

GLENN. That's the *phone*, Ken.

KEN. Why would he want a bone? It's a cat, not a dog.

(*The TELEPHONE rings again.*)

LENNY. I'll get it.

KEN. We're hungry, too, pussy. We haven't eaten either.

LENNY. (*Into phone.*) Hello? ... Who? ... I'm sorry, operator. We have a bad connection ... Oh, yes. Yes. (*To Others.*) It's Harry and Joan from Venezuela. They're calling Charley and Myra.

CLAIRE. This is going to be good.

GLENN. Joan? That's Cassie's cousin. Wait, I'll get Cassie. I'm sure she'll want to speak to her. (*HE knocks on the powder room door.*) Cassie?

LENNY. (*Into phone.*) Hello, Joannie. It's Lenny. How are you? ... Yes, everybody's here ... Yes, we're having a great time ...

GLENN. Cassie?

LENNY. (*Into phone.*) Charley and Myra? Of course they're here. What did you think? (*HE laughs and motions for CLAIRE and CHRIS to laugh, too.*) Sure. Just a minute. (*Covering the phone.*) Claire! Speak to her.

CLAIRE. Me? She's calling Charley and Myra.

LENNY. *Will you speak to her!!* (*HE shoves the phone at Claire.*)

GLENN. (*Knocking on the powder room door.*) Cassie? It's your cousin Joan from Venezuela.

CLAIRE. (*Into phone.*) Joan? What a nice surprise. No, it's Claire ... Yes, a terrific party ... Myra? Oh, she looks beautiful. She's wearing a red kimono. Mai Li's mother sent it to her ... Wait, I'll let you speak to her. Hold on. (*Covering the phone, to Chris.*) Here. Talk to her.

CHRIS. Don't give me the phone. I'll drive your kids to school for a year.

CLAIRE. (*Dumping the phone in Chris's lap.*) I've done my part. I'm not the Red Cross.

GLENN. (*Knocking on the powder room door.*) Cassie? It's Joan and Harry. Don't you want to speak to them?

CHRIS. (*Into phone.*) Joan? Hi, sweetheart. How's Venezuela? ... No, it's Chris. You sent a gift? A crystal vase from Steuben's? Gee, I think it's broken. Wait, Myra will tell you about it.

GLENN. (*Still knocking.*) Cassie, are you all right?

CHRIS. Who didn't speak to her yet?

CLAIRE. Ken. Ken didn't speak to her.

LENNY. (*Shouting at KEN, on the balcony.*) Ken? Do you want to speak to Joan?

KEN. What?

LENNY. *Joan! Do-you-want-to-speak-to-Joan?*

KEN. Sure. I'd love to go home.

CHRIS. (*Into phone.*) Joan? This connection is bad. I think I'm losing you.

GLENN. (*Banging on the bathroom door.*) Cassie, will you hurry up! We're losing the connection! *Come on, will you!!*

(*ERNIE and COOKIE come out of the kitchen. SHE holds a hot casserole, HE holds two bottles of wine.*)

COOKIE. It's din-din, everyone.

(*The bathroom door opens and CASSIE comes out in a state of shock.*)

CASSIE. *Who did that? Who banged on the door?*

GLENN. I did. Your cousin Joan is on the phone from Venezuela.

CASSIE. You scared the life out of me! I dropped my crystal down the toilet. A TWO-MILLION-YEAR-OLD CRYSTAL!!

CHRIS. I can't take this. (*SHE shoves the phone into Ken's hand.*) Here. You can't hear anyway, what's the difference?

(KEN holds the phone, bewildered. As SHE walks away, SHE trips on the phone wire and falls flat on her face.)

CASSIE. *(To Glenn.)* Don't just stand there, idiot, get my crystal.

GLENN. Hey, just cool it, Cassie, okay?

KEN. *(Into phone.)* Hello? ... Hello?

ERNIE. *(Starting up the stairs.)* I'll go get Myra and Charley.

LENNY. *(Dashing up the stairs, cutting off Ernie.)* No, I'll get them, I'll get them. Myra and Charley! Myra and Chaaaaa ... *(HE grabs his neck.)* Oh, shit! There it goes. This time it's permanent.

KEN. Hello? ... Hello? ...

CASSIE. *(Crying.)* It's a sin to lose a crystal. It's like killing your own dog.

LENNY. Oh, fuck a duck!

COOKIE. Everybody grab a plate, kids. *(As SHE hands out plates, her back goes out.)* Whoops. Oh, no. Oh, Christ. Oh, man. Oh, Momma.

KEN. Hello? ... Hello? ...

CURTAIN

ACT II

SCENE: One hour later.
Plates of eaten food are about. Opened wine and champagne
*   bottles are scattered about.*
It's quiet. Very quiet.

AT RISE: The only sound is of KEN eating. HE sits in an
*   armchair finishing his dinner. The OTHERS have all*
*   eaten. GLENN and CLAIRE are seated on the sofa.*
*   LENNY is on the love seat, drinking wine. COOKIE*
*   sits on a chair near KEN, drinking coffee. CASSIE is*
*   standing on the balcony, holding the rail with her*
*   hands and drawing in deep breaths. ERNIE and CHRIS*
*   sit on the stairway. CHRIS is smoking a cigarette,*
*   like it was her last, and ERNIE smokes a pipe.*
No one is talking. THEY are ALL deep in thought. NO
*   ONE looks at each other.*
The silence continues.
KEN's fork scratches on his plate as HE eats the last
*   morsel of food. HE looks up.*

KEN. (*Panicky.*) What was that?
GLENN. It was you, Ken. It was your fork scraping
the plate.
KEN. My what?
CHRIS. Your fork scraping your plate.
KEN. (*To Glenn.*) You're fading out again, Glenn.
GLENN. That wasn't me, Ken. It was Chris.

71

KEN. I can make out voices now. Just a little here and there.

CHRIS. (*To Ernie.*) You think I can have another cigarette?

KEN. No. No cigarettes.

GLENN. (*Crossing to Lenny at the love seat.*) I still can't get over it. I find the entire story so hard to believe.

LENNY. He finds the story hard to believe. Because we acted our asses off to keep the truth from you.

GLENN. Myra is gone?

LENNY. Right.

GLENN. The servants are gone?

LENNY. Right.

GLENN. Charley shoots himself in the ear lobe?

LENNY. Right.

GLENN. It doesn't make any sense.

CLAIRE, CHRIS, & LENNY. Right!

ERNIE. Why didn't I see it? People running up and down stairs, no one answering the door, cans of shaving cream exploding. I'm on the staff of Bellevue Hospital, how could I believe such a story? (*To Chris.*) You never let on.

CHRIS. Listen, I was so desperate for a smoke, I went into Charley's bathroom and tried to light up a Q-tip.

COOKIE. Don't you have any self-control?

CHRIS. Of course. I only smoked half.

(*KEN suddenly stands and looks around at everyone. HE is breathing hard and clenches his fists. HE looks as though HE's about to explode.*)

CHRIS. Something's wrong with Ken.

COOKIE. Maybe he's still hungry. YOU WANT
SECONDS, KENNY?

ERNIE. No, no. He wants to say something. Be quiet
a minute, everyone ... What is it, Ken?

KEN. I can't take it anymore ... The pressure is
killing me. I'm sorry, but I have to do this. (*To Ernie and
Glenn.*) Myra isn't here! The servants aren't here! Charley's
upstairs and he shot himself through the ear lobe! Maybe it
was attempted suicide, maybe it wasn't, I don't know. I
don't care. I'm just glad it's over with. (*HE sits back down
in his chair, sobbing.*)

ERNIE. It's all right, Ken. We know. Lenny told us.

KEN. (*Looking at him.*) You know?

ERNIE. Yes.

KEN. Who told you?

ERNIE. Lenny told us.

KEN. Glenn told you?

ERNIE. No. Lenny. LENNY. LENNY TOLD US.

CLAIRE. I wish he were deaf again.

KEN. (*Looks at Lenny.*) Is it true, Lenny? Did you
tell them?

LENNY. Oh, finish your goddam dinner and leave us
alone, will you?

ERNIE. All right, take it easy, Lenny. He's been
under a big strain.

LENNY. And I haven't? I was acting my goddam head
off that Myra was here. I had actual conversations with her
up there. I even did her voice in case someone was
listening.

COOKIE. Was that you? You could have fooled me.

LENNY. I *did*.

COOKIE. That's right. You did.

GLENN. So you really weren't watching Hitler on PBS?

LENNY. No, we stopped everything to watch "The Rise and Fall of Adolf Hitler" ... I don't believe you people.

GLENN. It sounded so real, I believed it.

ERNIE. (*To Cassie.*) What about you, Mrs. Cooper? (*To Glenn.*) What's her name?

GLENN. Cassie.

ERNIE. (*To Cassie.*) What about you, Cassie? Did you think something strange was going on?

CASSIE. Yes. For about six months now.

ERNIE. What do you mean? (*To Glenn.*) What does she mean?

GLENN. You have to forgive her. She's still very upset about losing her crystal.

COOKIE. We could call a plumber. They get everything out. Wedding rings, car keys. I had an aunt who lost her dentures down the toilet and they got them out.

CLAIRE. And she wore them?

COOKIE. Well, obviously you clean them.

CLAIRE. They could be blessed by the Pope, I wouldn't put them in my mouth again.

GLENN. Unless you're into crystals, you wouldn't understand. Apparently, they have very special properties. You have to wash them in clear, spring water. They must be kept in direct sunlight. Cassie scrubs them every night with a soft, wet toothbrush. You never dry them in a towel. You pat them in a sort of leathery cloth. They really are very delicate.

CLAIRE. Have you got them enrolled in a good school yet?

ERNIE. Oh, come on, Claire. If crystals work for her, if they give her a sense of comfort and pleasure, what's wrong with it?

CASSIE. You don't have to defend me, Ernie. Crystals will be here millions of years after this planet is gone.

LENNY. If the planet is gone, don't the crystals go with it?

ERNIE. Lenny, don't.

CHRIS. (*To Glenn.*) I don't know if this would help her any, but there's a big crystal chandelier in the dining room. Should I mention it to her?

GLENN. Thanks, Chris, but I don't think so. Best leave her alone now.

CASSIE. (*Coming downstairs.*) I'm not dead, you know. I can hear. Maybe Ken can't, but I can. (*SHE exits into the powder room.*)

COOKIE. I can unscrew the toilet myself. I've done it before.

ERNIE. I don't think it's the time or the place to fix toilets, sugar.

CLAIRE. Yes. Perhaps another time, another place.

LENNY. (*To Cookie.*) Bleeding arm and all, Cookie, that was one hell of a meal. My hat's off to you.

GLENN. Hear hear.

ERNIE. Bravissima.

CHRIS. Arregeno! Arregeno!

EVERYBODY. I liked the duck. The duck was great. Really crispy. And the pasta was especially good. Didn't you think so? How long did you boil it?

KEN. (*Gets up with that mad look on his face again.*) Doesn't anybody ... doesn't *anybody*—?

ERNIE. Quiet, everybody. Quiet ... What is it, Ken? Doesn't anybody what?

KEN. Doesn't anybody – want to go upstairs and see if Charley is still alive? It's been awfully quiet up there, hasn't it?

CLAIRE. How would you know?

KEN. What?

ERNIE. You're right. My God, he's right. We've all been so busy eating and explaining to each other, we forgot all about Charley.

KEN. (*Pointing to Ernie.*) YES. *YES.* That's what I'm saying.

LENNY. All right, I'll go up and settle this now.

GLENN. Wait, wait. We're all in a precarious situation. Not only Charley, but a lot of people's futures depend on how we deal with this issue.

CLAIRE. Meaning you?

GLENN. Well, no. Cassie and I were the last ones to arrive. We just heard about it. We're hardly involved.

COOKIE. And Ernie and I were cooking the whole time. Nobody told us. Sorry.

LENNY. I *wanted* to call the police. Ken wouldn't let me call the police. Claire, didn't I want to call the police?

CLAIRE. Lenny wanted to call the police.

CHRIS. So what are you saying? That it's Ken's responsibility? He takes the rap for this?

ALL THE OTHERS. Oh, no. No, of course not ... We didn't say that ... Nobody's saying that. I didn't hear anyone say that. No one's accusing anyone of anything.

LENNY. ... What we're saying is, if it comes down to it, he's the most logical, that's all.

CHRIS. I can't believe this. Ken almost went deaf trying to protect Charley and everyone else here. I expected a little bit more from his friends. My God, what a bunch of wimps ... Have you heard any of this, Ken?

KEN. Well, answer her, Glenn, have you?

COOKIE. (*Screams, as SHE bends way over.*) Oh, God! Oh, no! Oh, Christ! Oh, Momma!

LENNY. What is it?

COOKIE. I lost my earrings. My good earrings! My grandmother's earrings!

CHRIS. (*Bending over, looking.*) Where did you lose them?

COOKIE. Right here. Right around here.

ERNIE. We'll find them, honey.

CLAIRE. What did they look like?

COOKIE. Old! Very old! With pearls. And a little ruby. (*Starting to cry.*) My grandmother gave them to me. I'm sick about this.

(*THEY are ALL on the floor, crawling around looking for the earrings.*)

COOKIE. (*Screams.*) AHHHH! Oh, God! Oh, my God!

CLAIRE. What?

COOKIE. They're in my hand. (*Shows them.*) I forgot I had them. I'm so stupid. Forgive me, everybody, I'm sorry ... So, what were we saying?

(*THEY ALL glare at Cookie as THEY struggle to their feet.*)

ERNIE. Glenn, I'm a little worried about your wife. Do you think she's all right.

GLENN. Oh, she's fine. She's just in there trying to figure some way to get back at me. She'll come up with something.

(*The powder room door suddenly opens and CASSIE stands there with one arm extended up the door. Her hair is brushed over one eye. SHE looks sexy as hell, with a malevolent grin on her face. EVERYONE turns to look at her.*)

GLENN. Yeah, she's got one.

(*CASSIE crosses to the sofa, sits on the arm next to Lenny, practically leaning on him.*)

CASSIE. Please forgive me, everyone. I know I behaved badly tonight.

(*SHE smiles right at Lenny. HE smiles back, then looks away.*)

CASSIE. No, I really did ... and I apologize. I've had – well, I've had a rough day today, and I'm just not here tonight.
LENNY. That's okay. Neither are Charley and Myra.
CASSIE. (*Smiles at Lenny.*) That's funny. That's truly funny, Lenny. I can never think of anything funny. How do you do that?
LENNY. (*A bit flustered.*) I don't know ... I just ... (*Sees CLAIRE glaring at him.*) Can I get up and get you a glass of wine?
CASSIE. Why? Do I look like I need one?

CLAIRE. Who is she getting back at, Glenn, you or me?

GLENN. (*Without looking at her.*) All right, Cassie, cut it out.

CASSIE. What do you mean, sweetheart.

GLENN. You know what I mean. Push your hair back up and sit on a chair.

CASSIE. (*Smiles at Glenn, then to Lenny.*) Do you know what he's talking about, Len?

CLAIRE. Excuse me. I'm going up to get Charley's gun.

ERNIE. Cassie, everyone here is your friend. Why don't you and I go out on the terrace and have a nice, quiet talk?

COOKIE. (*To Ernie.*) You do and you'll have a back worse than mine.

CASSIE. Oh, my goodness, I see what you're thinking. That is really incredible. Because the exact same thing happened to Glenn and me last week at a cocktail party for the Democratic Fund Raising Committee. There was the nicest woman there – very attractive, very sweet, very refined – and because sometimes I can feel so silly and so insecure, I thought she was coming on to Glenn. They got up to dance and they were as close as freshly-laid wallpaper.

GLENN. Okay, Cassie, I think we're going.

(*The INTERCOM on the phone buzzes.*)

KEN. (*Holding his chest.*) Excuse me. I must have eaten too quickly.

CHRIS. That was the intercom, Ken. Not you.

LENNY. (*Crossing to the phone.*) I'll get it. (*Picking up the phone.*) Hello? ... Charley? Are you all right? (*To others.*) It's Charley.

KEN. Molly? Who's Molly?

GLENN. (*Losing it.*) CHARLEY! CHARLEY! NOT MOLLY!

LENNY. (*Into phone.*) Yes, Charley, we're all here ... Len, Glenn, Ken, Ernie, Claire, Chris, Cassie, and Cookie.

CLAIRE. Isn't that odd that all the women's names begin with a C?

CHRIS. That's right.

COOKIE. Except Myra.

CHRIS. Her middle name is Clara.

CLAIRE. And the men's names are all the same. Len, Glenn, Ken.

CHRIS. That's right.

CLAIRE. Except for Ernie and Charley.

COOKIE. Charley begins with a C.

ERNIE. What is this, anagrams, for pete sakes? Let him talk on the phone.

LENNY. Yes, Charley, I understand. No, it's perfectly reasonable. You do what you have to do ... We'll be here. (*HE hangs up.*) He needs time to think.

KEN. More time to drink? He shouldn't drink with Valium.

GLENN. (*Shouting into Ken's ear.*) THINK! THINK! NOT DRINK.

KEN. Oh! Oh, my God! Oh, Jesus!

CHRIS. What? What is it?

KEN. My ears popped! They just opened up. My God, it sounds like a subway in here.

ERNIE. This is remarkable, but I'm having the first headache I've ever had in my life.

COOKIE. I just remembered.

CLAIRE. What?

COOKIE. Ernie's last name is Cusack. It begins with a C.

CLAIRE. You just remembered your husband's last name?

KEN. I can hear my own pulse. It's slightly up, but not too bad.

CASSIE. (*Smiles sexily at Ken.*) Can I take it, Ken? I'm very good at things like that.

GLENN. I'm warning you, Cassie. You're going to end up in the same place where your crystal is.

CASSIE. Don't threaten me, sweetheart, because I'll start naming names.

GLENN. That's it! That's it! I've got to stay, but I'm putting you in a taxi.

CASSIE. (*Screams.*) Never mind! I'LL WALK.

(*KEN grabs his ears in pain and drops to the floor. CASSIE storms out the front door.*)

GLENN. Walk? Twenty-two miles? Cassie, wait for me. Will you wait!! (*HE runs out after Cassie.*)

CLAIRE. I feel badly for her. Especially because one day she'll grow old and die.

COOKIE. I just thought of something else. Glenn went to Penn.

CHRIS. Oh, sit on it, will you, honey.

ERNIE. If I had you all in my group, I would never need another group again.

KEN. (*At the Stage Right wall, near the window.*) Shh. Quiet. I can hear them.

LENNY. Hear who?

KEN. Glenn and Cassie. They're in the driveway. I swear, I can hear them talking.

CLAIRE. The man is a German shepherd.

ERNIE. I don't think it's your business to listen, Ken.

LENNY. If he can hear through walls, it's his business.

KEN. She's talking about a woman. She's very upset.

COOKIE. (*Looking out the window.*) I'll say. She just kicked a car with her foot. Who owns the BMW?

LENNY. Ah, shit. The good side too, I bet.

CHRIS. (*Leaping to her feet.*) I just figured it out.

CLAIRE. I know what she's going to say. Glenn, Ken and Len are all men.

CHRIS. No, no, no. It's Glenn Cooper ... Glenn is the one that Myra's having the affair with.

COOKIE. You think so.

CHRIS. Figure it out. Myra's been working very hard on Glenn's campaign. Two, three nights a week. *Late* nights.

CLAIRE. Of course. Charley's not dumb. He puts two and two together, confronts Myra with it, she confesses, Charley kicks her out of the house, tells the servants to go home and tries to blow his brains out.

ERNIE. You don't know that. That's an assumption on your part. That is a very, very dangerous statement to make. Don't you agree with me, Len?

LENNY. No.

ERNIE. Why not?

LENNY. I don't feel like it.

ERNIE. Listen, I think we have to bring this thing to a head. I'm going to go up and speak to Charley and find out what's what. (*HE starts for the stairs.*)

KEN. Wait a minute. Hold it! As far as Charley's concerned, only Chris and I know about Charley shooting himself in the ear, am I right?

LENNY. Right. He never said a word to me. He had the pillow covering up his ear the whole time.

CLAIRE. So what you're saying is, he doesn't know we know anything.

ERNIE. Well, he's got to know that we all haven't seen Myra. And that there's no servants here.

KEN. Exactly. But he doesn't know the *rest* of you know about the gunshot.

CHRIS. Slower. Go slower. Talk like we're children.

KEN. My point is, I told him we wouldn't tell anybody.

CLAIRE. And then you went ahead and told everybody.

KEN. No, no. I told only you and Lenny. Lenny told everybody.

LENNY. But you were deaf then. You didn't hear me telling everybody.

CLAIRE. (*To Ken.*) And then you told everybody *after* Lenny told everybody.

CHRIS. Go fast again. It doesn't make any difference.

(*COOKIE stands up and goes to the window.*)

KEN. What I'm trying to say is, as long as Charley doesn't think the rest of you know —

ERNIE. — why tell him now? I see your point. We've got to keep up the subterfuge. If we confront him with everyone knowing about the gunshot, he could go to pieces. So until he tells us his own story himself, we have to pretend we don't know anything.

KEN. I should be the one who goes up. I tell Charley
that everyone is here. And he asks me does everyone know
what's happened.

ERNIE. You say, "No."

KEN. I say, "No." Then Charley asks me, well, if I'm
not down there and Myra's not down there and the help's
not down there, what did you tell them?

COOKIE. (*Looking out the window.*) Something's
wrong with Cassie. Woops.

LENNY. Woops? What's woops? She threw up in the
car?

COOKIE. She hit Glenn. His nose is bleeding.

CLAIRE. Tell me when he hits her back. I'd love to
watch that.

KEN. Will you all please be quiet. I can't hear myself
think. What was I saying?

CHRIS. (*Quickly.*) You said, "I should be the one
who goes up. I tell Charley that everyone is here." And he
asks "Does everyone here know what's happened?" Ernie
said, "You say, 'No.'" You said, "I say no." Then Charley
asks me, "Well, if I'm not down there and Myra's not
down there —"

KEN. Allrightallrightallright!!

ERNIE. I've got it. I've got it. Here's what we do.
Charley's going to want to know what Ken told us. Ken
tells Charley that he told us that Charley had a large benign
wart removed from his ear this morning, but he's okay.
Then suddenly Myra's mother broke her hip this afternoon
and that Myra took her to the hospital and is going to stay
there the night. The help, thinking the party was off, left
the food and went home. It all happened so fast, they forgot
to call us. We all got here, we understood and decided to
cook the dinner ourselves ... That's the story.

CLAIRE. I wouldn't believe the mother breaking her hip.

ERNIE. Why not?

CLAIRE. She died six years ago.

ERNIE. Then her father broke his hip.

CLAIRE. Her father lives in California.

ERNIE. Does she have a relative in the city?

CHRIS. She has a cousin Florence.

ERNIE. Then Florence broke her hip.

CHRIS. Florence is married. Why didn't her husband take her?

ERNIE. Then Myra broke her hip. The neighbors took her.

COOKIE. If he only had a wart removed, Charley could have taken her.

CLAIRE. Can't you think of something else?

ERNIE. (*Upset.*) *I did!* I thought of the mother, the father, the cousin, the wart and the hip. Nothing satisfies you people.

KEN. There's no logic to it. Nothing in that story is plausible.

ERNIE. (*Losing it.*) We don't need plausible. The man is in shock, mental anguish and emotional despair. Logic doesn't mean shit to him right now. (*He sits down, composes himself.*) Excuse my language.

(*The PHONE rings. THEY ALL look at it. The PHONE rings again. THEY ALL look at each other.*)

ERNIE. The telephone!

LENNY. Don't you think we know it's a telephone? We all have telephones, Ernie. We're all wealthy people here.

(*The PHONE is still ringing.*)

ERNIE. Just calm down, everybody. (*HE picks up the phone.*) Hello? ... Yes? ... Yes, he is ... Who's calling, please? ... I see. All right ... Just a moment, please. (*Covering the phone.*) It's a woman. For Glenn.

CLAIRE. So?

ERNIE. It sounds like Myra.

COOKIE. Oh, fuck-a-doodle-doo.

KEN. Should I go get him?

ERNIE. Wait a minute. (*Into phone.*) Er, Glenn is outside just now. Can I tell him who's calling? ... I see. All right. Hold on. (*Covering the phone.*) I can't tell. Maybe it is, maybe it isn't.

COOKIE. What did she say when you asked who's calling?

ERNIE. She said, "Just a friend."

LENNY. How did she say it?

ERNIE. She said, "Just a friend." How many ways are there to say it?

LENNY. I'll tell you how many ways. Nervous, phony, sincere, drunk –

CHRIS. Scared, guilty, lying –

COOKIE. Off-handed, perplexed, deceitful –

CLAIRE. Ominous, anonymous –

ERNIE. THIS ISN'T SCRABBLE, for God's sakes.

LENNY. Let me talk to her.

ERNIE. She didn't ask for you.

LENNY. She didn't ask for you, either. I know Myra's voice. Give me the phone. (*HE grabs the phone from Ernie.*) Hello? ... No, it isn't. It's Glenn's friend, Len ... No, Ken is getting Glenn ... You sound awfully familiar.

Do I know you? ... I see ... Well, hold on, please. (*Covering the phone.*) I don't think it's her.

COOKIE. Well, who does it sound like?

LENNY. Meryl Streep.

COOKIE. Meryl Streep? Why would Meryl Streep call here?

LENNY. I didn't say it *was* Meryl Streep. But you know how she sounds in the movies? Like she always does the character perfectly but it's not really her. That's how she sounds.

COOKIE. Like she's not Meryl Streep?

ERNIE. Now we're playing "Trivial Pursuit!" This is not a game show. Ken, will you please get Glenn? (*Grabbing the phone from Lenny.*) Hello? ... Somebody went to get Glenn ... Hello? ... (*HE hangs up.*) She hung up. She must have gotten suspicious.

KEN. Quiet down everyone. I hear something!

CLAIRE. I'll bet it's the Concorde landing in London.

KEN. It's a car coming up the driveway.

(*HEADLIGHTS flash on the window.*)

CLAIRE. Maybe it's Myra.

LENNY. Maybe it's Harry and Joan from Venezuela.

(*The front door opens quickly and GLENN rushes in holding a bloody hanky to his nose.*)

GLENN. We got trouble. Oh, God, have we got trouble.

KEN. What is it?

GLENN. The police. It's a police car.

LENNY. (*Loudly, pointing at Ken.*) Okay! I warned you! I *told* you we should have called the police. Now look what's happened. The police came.

KEN. Who could have called the police?

CLAIRE. Maybe it was Myra.

CHRIS. Maybe it was Charley.

LENNY. Maybe it was Cassie. (*To Glenn.*) You were fighting with her, weren't you? Did she use the phone in my car?

GLENN. Not to call. She hit me with it.

LENNY. She broke my phone? My new phone in my new car?

ERNIE. Will everybody calm down. We've got to figure out what to say when they come in.

COOKIE. (*Looking out the window.*) They're trying to talk to Cassie. She won't roll down the windows.

LENNY. *My* windows? They're going to bust my windows? I'm going to take my car home in an envelope.

ERNIE. (*To Glenn.*) Why did you leave her out there in the car? She's in no condition to answer police questions.

GLENN. She's in good enough condition to smash my nose ... Goddam, I got blood on my shirt.

LENNY. And you're running for the State Senate? I wouldn't let you run for Chinese food.

CHRIS. What's wrong with you people? I've got a six-year-old child at home who behaves better than we do.

LENNY. Fine! Then get him over here and tell *him* to talk to the police.

KEN. Take it easy, Len. She's been doing her share. She's the one who called Dr. Dudley.

LENNY. EVERYBODY CALLED DR. DUDLEY. HE'S IN THE YELLOW PAGES IN CHINA!!

CLAIRE. Maybe Dudley called the police.

(*The TELEPHONE rings.*)

ERNIE. It's the phone again.

LENNY. He's right. He guessed it was the phone twice in a row. This genius is going to save our lives.

ERNIE. (*Picking up the phone.*) Hello? ... Yes? ... Just a minute, please. (*To Glenn.*) Glenn, it's for you. (*Announcing to the Group.*) It's the same woman who called before.

GLENN. (*Crossing to the phone.*) What same woman?

CLAIRE. She wouldn't say. Maybe it was Myra, maybe it was Meryl Streep.

GLENN. Meryl Streep?

CLAIRE. You know how she sounds in the movies? Like she always does the character perfectly, but it's not really her? That's how this person sounded.

LENNY. (*At the front door, looking out.*) We've got two policemen coming in, she's giving us a resume of the party.

COOKIE. (*Looking out the window.*) Oh, oh. They're walking over here.

GLENN. (*Into phone.*) Hello?

COOKIE. (*Hobbling away from the window.*) They're on the way over.

GLENN. (*Into phone.*) Oh, hi. How are you? ... No, it's not a cold, it's a telephone injury.

KEN. Now listen. The thing we can't do is let them see Charley. We can't let him downstairs or them upstairs.

GLENN. (*Into phone.*) I tried talking to Cassie, but she's very upset.

ERNIE. (*Gesturing importantly.*) Above all, no false statements. We must keep within the law. This above all, agreed?

LENNY. (*Mocking Ernie's gestures.*) Yea! To thine own self be true. Wherein the hearts of better men – are you fucking crazy? They're outside the door.

GLENN. (*Into phone.*) Of course I think you should talk to her, but I can't get her out of the car.

KEN. They're going to ask about the gunshots. What do we tell them about the gunshots?

GLENN. (*Into phone.*) All right, I'll call you back in fifteen minutes. Are you at the nine-one-four number?

LENNY. Kill him! Somebody kill him! Choke him with the telephone wire.

(*The DOORBELL chimes.*)

CHRIS. I'm very serious about this, but I'm not going to be able to hold my bladder.

ERNIE. All right, I've got it. We tell them we never ! :ard the gunshots.

CLAIRE. You mean lie to them?

LENNY. What happened to "this above all?"

ERNIE. It won't work tonight. Maybe some other time.

CHRIS. If you let me go to the bathroom, I promise I'll come back.

GLENN. (*Still on the phone.*) Listen, I know you're a good friend. And I thank you for all your wonderful support.

LENNY. Leave him here. Let's run for our lives and leave that schmuck for the cops.

GLENN. (*Into phone.*) I can't talk anymore. I'll call you back later ... I will ... Goodbye. (*Hangs up and turns to the others.*) All right, what's going on?

LENNY. Well, about six weeks ago we got an invitation to this party –

ERNIE. Stop it, Lenny ... All right, think everybody. Think. Why didn't we hear the gunshots?

COOKIE. (*Raising her hand.*) We're all deaf people. We meet once a week. That's why we didn't hear the doorbell.

LENNY. (*To Claire.*) Now you know why they cal her Cookie.

CHRIS. I've got it! We were listening to the Hitler program. The cannons were bombing Berlin, we couldn't hear anything else.

(*THEY all consider.*)

LENNY. THERE WAS NO HITLER PROGRAM. WE MADE THE FUCKING THING UP TO FOOL THIS ASSHOLE. (*Points to Glenn.*)

GLENN. Hey, I've had just about enough from you, Lenny.

(*The DOORBELL chimes. ALL drop to the floor.*)

KEN. We've got to let them in.

LENNY. All right. Claire, open the door.

CLAIRE. I can't. I'm in charge of the music.

GLENN. The music! That's it!

CHRIS. What is?

GLENN. The music was on. We were all dancing. We couldn't hear the gunshots. Claire, put on the music.

(*CLAIRE goes to the stereo cabinet.*)

KEN. (*To Claire.*) WAIT!! Don't turn it on yet. There's one last thing to do.

CLAIRE. What?

KEN. Somebody has to be Charley. Just in case.

LENNY. Just in case what?

KEN. Just in case the police want to speak to Charley.

ERNIE. Ken is right. Charley is in no condition to tell them the real story.

LENNY. Of course not, because no one has *heard* the real story yet.

KEN. Exactly. But we have to be sure whatever story the police hear, has to be one that's not going to get us all in trouble.

CHRIS. I never saw a sinking ship empty so fast.

GLENN. I agree. Ken is absolutely right. (*To the Men.*) One of you three guys has to be Charley.

LENNY. When did *you* move to France?

GLENN. Well, let's be honest. I never even heard the gunshots.

LENNY. (*Shouting in Glenn's ear.*) BANG BANG, you bastard!

COOKIE. Isn't it against the law to impersonate another real person?

ERNIE. Yes, it is dear, but not if you do it well.

CHRIS. (*To the Women.*) Can you believe we actually married these men?

LENNY. This is a major felony we're talking about. You want to spend thirty years in a maximum security prison wearing a tuxedo?

KEN. (*Coming downstage and taking charge.*) We're all in this together, Glenn. Here's how we do it. You put out two fingers or one finger. If three guys are the same and one is different, that guy is Charley ... Are we ready?

LENNY. Who made you Don Corleone?

KEN. You have a better idea?

LENNY. Yeah. Let the women wrestle for it.

GLENN. Come on. Let's get it over with, for crise sakes.

KEN. Okay. Here we go. One – two – three!

(*The MEN put out fingers.*)

KEN. Two and two. No good ... Try again. Ready? One – two – three!

(*The MEN put out fingers.*)

KEN. All the same. No good ... Again!

(*The DOORBELL rings.*)

KEN. Ready one – two – three!

(*The MEN put out fingers.*)

KEN. Aha! Lenny!

LENNY. (*Quickly putting his hand behind his back.*) What do you mean, Lenny?

GLENN. We all have two fingers out, you have one finger.

LENNY. Bullshit! I had two stuck together. (*HE shows them.*) I got duck grease on my fingers.

ERNIE. It was one finger, Lenny.

LENNY. It was two, I swear to God.

ERNIE. No, no. It was one. ONE FINGER. ONE! I SAW IT!!

COOKIE. And that man graduated from Johns Hopkins.

GLENN. Go on upstairs, Lenny. And don't come down unless we call you.

LENNY. No, I'm anxious to come as Charley. (*HE goes into Charley's room and closes the door.*)

(*The DOORBELL rings again.*)

KEN. Okay, Claire, put on the music.

ERNIE. Let's go, kids. Hurry up. Get your partners.

(*THEY do.*)

ERNIE. Okay.

(*CLAIRE turns on the stereo. It is a loud rendition of "La Bamba" ... the THREE COUPLES dance furiously.*

We hear loud BANGING on the front door, and then it is opened.

TWO POLICEMEN stand there. One, OFFICER WELCH, a strong, vigorous man. The other, OFFICER PUDNEY, is a woman in her late twenties.

THEY stand watching the COUPLES dance. NO ONE seems to notice the POLICE.)

WELCH. (*Yells.*) Can you shut that thing off, please!

(*NO ONE notices.*)

WELCH. SOMEBODY PLEASE SHUT THAT DAMN THING OFF!

(*KEN turns the MUSIC off. THEY ALL look surprised that the Police are in the room.*)

ERNIE. (*Indignant.*) I beg your pardon. May I ask what you're doing here?

WELCH. I'm sorry. I didn't mean to bust the door open.

ERNIE. Then why didn't you ring first?

WELCH. I did. Five times.

ERNIE. (*Crossing near the Police.*) Five times? We didn't hear it.

WELCH. I guess the music was on so loud, you couldn't hear anything.

ERNIE. Of *course*. The *music*.

KEN. That's why we didn't hear you.

CLAIRE. No wonder we didn't get any phone calls. We wouldn't hear them.

CHRIS. That's what it was. The music.

COOKIE. It was on ...

ALL. ... *so loud*.

ERNIE. (*Congenial.*) Now, what seems to be the trouble, officer?

WELCH. Well, just sort of routine investigation, sir. My name is Officer Welch. This is Officer Pudney. Is this your house, sir?

ERNIE. *My* house? No, no. I live elsewhere. Other than here.

KEN. As I do. Live elsewhere. Could you tell us what this is about, officer?

EVERYONE. Yes, what's this about? Is anything wrong? Why are the police here? I can't imagine what's going on.

WELCH. All right, all right, take it easy. Calm down. I just want to ask a few questions ... May I ask who the owner of this house is?

KEN. We'd be delighted to tell, Officer, but I believe it's customary first for you to inform us as to why these questions are being asked of us.

WELCH. You're a lawyer, aren't you.

KEN. Yes, I am.

WELCH. Well, as a lawyer you understand you're not obligated to answer these questions. I was hoping someone would be cooperative enough to tell me the owner's name.

(*THEY ALL look at each other.*)

CLAIRE. Brock. Charley Brock.

WELCH. Could you tell me if Mr. Brock is at home at present?

(*THEY ALL look at each other.*)

CLAIRE. I'm not sure. Chris, is Charley at home?

CHRIS. Charley? I think he went to walk the dog.

WELCH. Then he'll be back soon?

COOKIE. I don't think so. It's a Dachshund. They take very small steps.

KEN. (*Wanting no trouble.*) He's home. He came back, Officer.

WELCH. Well, then could I possible see Mr. Brock for a moment?

KEN. (*Coming Downstage, taking charge.*) Well, it's an awkward time, Officer. As you can see, we're celebrating a party.

WELCH. Yes, I've noticed. What's the occasion?

KEN. The tenth wedding anniversary of Charley and Myra Brock.

WELCH. (*Crossing to Ken.*) I wouldn't take long. I just need a minute of his time.

KEN. Well, unfortunately, Mr. Brock is sleeping.

WELCH. Sleeping? In the middle of his anniversary party?

KEN. He was feeling depressed. He took a sleeping pill.

WELCH. Well, could I see *Mrs.* Brock?

KEN. Mrs. Brock is not here.

WELCH. She's not?

KEN. That's why Mr. Brock is depressed.

WELCH. Where is she?

(*THEY ALL look at each other.*)

ERNIE. ... Her father broke his hip. She had to take him to the hospital.

(*THEY ALL glare at him.*)

WELCH. During her anniversary party? Couldn't someone *else* take him to the hospital?

CLAIRE. Her father lives in California.

CHRIS. It has to do with cousins and warts and hips. It's very complicated.

WELCH. (*Crossing to GLENN who is hiding his face with his hand.*) You, sir? Something wrong with your eye?

GLENN. Me? Yes. I put some drops in tonight and the cap fell off. Most of the bottle went in.

WELCH. May I have your name, sir?

GLENN. My name?

WELCH. Yes, sir.

GLENN. You mean, my name?

WELCH. Yes, sir ... Is there a problem with giving me your name?

GLENN. I'm sorry. I just can't see you very well.

WELCH. You don't have to see to talk, sir. The drops didn't go in your mouth, did they?

KEN. Officer, I feel you're being unnecessarily abusive to these people. If you're going to ask any more questions, you'll have to tell us what this is all about.

WELCH. Yes, sir. I will ... Can you please tell me who owns the BMW outside?

CLAIRE. It's my husband's car.

WELCH. And what is his name, please?

KEN. You don't have to answer that, Claire.

CLAIRE. His name is Len. Leonard Ganz.

WELCH. And where is Mr. Ganz now?

KEN. (*Like in court.*) I object.

WELCH. (*Annoyed.*) I ain't a judge! This ain't a court! I don't have a gavel! I just want to know where the man is.

KEN. You still haven't told us what this is about, so we're still not telling you where Mr. Ganz is.

WELCH. I don't know why I always have trouble in this neighborhood ... Okay ... (*Consulting his notebook.*) At approximately eight-fifteen tonight, an auto accident occurred on Twelfth and Danbury. A brand new red 1990 Porsche convertible with New York license plates, smashed into the side of a brand new BMW four-door sedan. Now, we know it wasn't the BMW's fault because the Porsche was a stolen car. Stolen at eight-fifteen tonight right off the dealer's lot. The man and the Porsche got away. Now do you know who that brand new Porsche belonged to?

CLAIRE. How would I know?

WELCH. It belonged to Deputy Mayor Charles M. Brock. Purchased today as a gift from his wife, Myra. A surprise wedding anniversary present.

CLAIRE. Surprise hardly says it.

KEN. Aha! So, you're here to investigate the car accident?

WELCH. That's right. Now if Mr. Ganz is here, I'd like to speak to him. And if he's not here, the police department would like to know where he is.

KEN. I see ... Do you think you could wait outside for one moment, officer?

WELCH. Why?

KEN. Mrs. Ganz is my client. I would like to consult with her before any further questioning. It's within my rights.

WELCH. ... One minute. That's all you get.

(WELCH motions to PUDNEY and THEY BOTH go out the front door.)

KEN. All right, we don't have much time. One of us has to be Lenny.

ERNIE. What are you talking about?

KEN. The man doesn't even know about the gunshots. He just wants to ask Lenny about the accident. But Lenny can't be Lenny because we need Lenny to be Charley in case he wants to ask Charley about the new car, and we can't let him see Charley because Charley has a bullet hole in his ear.

COOKIE. (*To Chris.*) Do you understand him in real life?

CHRIS. We don't actually talk that much.

KEN. All right. Glenn! Ernie! We have to choose again.

ERNIE. Oh, leave me alone with this stupid game. (*Walks away.*)

KEN. I know it's stupid, but we have to do it. We need a Lenny.

CHRIS. (*To Boys.*) Never mind. The girls will do it. Come on, girls. The odd woman's husband is Lenny.

CLAIRE. My husband *is* Lenny.

CHRIS. No, Lenny is Charley. You're playing for Glenn. Get in a circle.

(*THEY bunch together, just like the Men.*)

COOKIE. I don't know how to play this.

CHRIS. Just put out your fingers. We'll do the counting ... Odd finger loses ... All right? Ready? One – two – three.

(*The GIRLS puts out fingers except COOKIE who puts out a fist.*)

CHRIS. No! ... No no no no! Your fingers, Cookie, open your fist.

COOKIE. I don't want to lose my earrings again.

CHRIS. Just one or two fingers! All right? Here we go. One – two – three!

(*The GIRLS put out fingers.*)

CHRIS. Aha! It's me! Fuck! ... Sorry, Ken.
KEN. It's okay. All right, I'm Lenny. Open the door, Ernie.

(*ERNIE crosses to the front door. The front door opens. WELCH and PUDNEY come in. WELCH is unhappy.*)

WELCH. I'm glad to see you're not dancing again. Now where is Mr. Leonard Ganz?
KEN. He's right here in this room. I am Leonard Ganz.
WELCH. (*Looking at him sideways.*) *You* are?
KEN. Yes.
WELCH. How come it took you a whole minute to think of your name?
KEN. Never rush your answers. Harvard Law School.
WELCH. Never trust a man who doesn't know if he's here or not. Police Academy.

(*CHRIS involuntarily puts her arm through Ken's to protect him. WELCH sees this.*)

WELCH. Who are you, m'am?
CHRIS. I'm his wife. His wife's best friend. (*Pointing to Claire.*) Her. Mrs. Ganz. (*Takes her arm away.*)
WELCH. Are you here alone, m'am?
CHRIS. No. I'm here with my husband. Mr. Gorman.
WELCH. Where is he?
CHRIS. (*Looks around.*) Must have gone home early.
WELCH. Not much of a party, is it?

CHIRS. It's had it's up and downs.

WELCH. (*To Ken.*) All right, Mr. Ganz. Tell us about the accident. In full and complete detail.

KEN. ... Do you think you could step outside just one more time?

WELCH. I AIN'T GOING NO PLACE NO WHERE NO TIME!!! THIS IS IT!! This is where I live till I get what I came for, even if my whole family has to move in.

(*We hear the WALKIE-TALKIE squawk in Pudney's holster.*)

WELCH. What's that?

PUDNEY. 1047 Pudney. Over ... (*The RADIO squawks at her.*) Check ... Got it ... Hold it. (*To Welch.*) Red 1990 Porsche convertible located at Fifth and Market in Tarrytown. Suspect apprehended. They said call it a night.

WELCH. (*Nods.*) Well, I guess that ties that little bundle up.

EVERYBODY. Isn't that wonderful? Terrific! I'm so happy.

WELCH. Sorry to disturb you, folks.

EVERYBODY. Hey, it's okay. No problem. We understand.

WELCH. There'll be some further questioning for you tomorrow, Mr. Ganz. No need to take any more of your time tonight. Thank you and goodnight, folks.

EVERYONE. It's okay. Our pleasure. Anytime, officer.

(*GLENN goes to Welch and shakes his hand.*)

WELCH. I *know* I've seen you some place before. What's your name again?

GLENN. (*Happily.*) Glenn. Glenn Cooper.

WELCH. Were you ever on TV?

GLENN. Well, as a matter of fact, yes. I'm running for the State Senate.

WELCH. Right. I saw you do an interview on PBS.

WELCH. Why were you so afraid to give me your name?

GLENN. Well, you know. When you're in politics, you don't want to get mixed up with these things.

WELCH. Yes, but you weren't involved with this. Unless you witnessed the accident. Did you?

GLENN. No, no, no. My wife and I arrived late. We didn't even hear the gunshots.

(*A moment of frozen silence. The OTHERS look to heaven for help.*)

WELCH. ... What gunshots?

GLENN. Hmmm?

WELCH. I said, what gunshots?

GLENN. I suppose the gunshots that were fired when they chased the stolen car?

WELCH. That was twelve miles away over in Tarrytown. You got twenty-twenty hearing, Mr. Cooper?

(*PUDNEY's WALKIE-TALKIE squawks again.*)

PUDNEY. 1047 Pudney. Over ... (*SHE listens. It SQUAWKS.*) Right ... Check ... Will do. (*SHE turns it off. To Welch.*) Neighbors reported two gunshots were fired

about nine P.M. from inside 1257 Peekskill Road,
Sneden's Landing. Investigate.

WELCH. 1257 Peekskill Road ... Well, we've got
ourselves a double header, don't we? ... Anybody want to
tell us about the gunshots?

EVERYBODY. No. Not really. We didn't hear any
gunshots. The music was so loud.

WELCH. Nobody heard them, I suppose. (*To Glenn.*)
Who's the woman sitting outside in the BMW?

GLENN. She's my wife, Cassie.

WELCH. I'd like to have a little talk with Mrs.
Cooper ... Connie, get her in here.

COOKIE. (*Portentously.*) Connie? With a C?

(*PUDNEY exits through the front door.*)

WELCH. (*Coming downstage.*) Looks to me like you
all had a fine dinner ... I'd like to speak to the help, please.

KEN. There is no help.

WELCH. Then who did the cooking?

COOKIE. I did.

WELCH. What's your name?

COOKIE. Cookie.

WELCH. I mean your real name.

COOKIE. That *is* my real name. I have two sisters
named Candy and Taffy. I swear to God.

WELCH. (*Looks at Ken.*) Is that blood on your shirt,
Len.

KEN. Blood? Oh, yes. I cut myself with a fork during
dinner.

WELCH. (*Nods doubtingly, looks at Glenn.*) Is that
blood on *your* shirt, Glenn?

GLENN. Oh, yes. I must have rubbed against Len ... when we were dancing.

WELCH. Ken, Len, and Glenn. That's really weird.

KEN. It's just a coincidence.

WELCH. I guess it is. My name is Ben.

(The front door opens, and CASSIE comes in with PUDNEY. CASSIE is still angry. The shoulder pad on her suit jacket has been ripped open at the seam, and the white padding hangs out.)

WELCH. Are you all right, Mrs. Cooper?

CASSIE. I'm not pressing any charges. My lawyer will handle this.

GLENN. It was an accident. She dropped the electric cigarette lighter in the car on the leather seat, and I grabbed her jacket to pull her out of the car.

WELCH. (*To Glenn.*) And how'd you get that nasty blow on your nose?

GLENN. My wife was hanging up the car phone in the dark and my head was a little too low.

WELCH. My my my. We got a lot of cartoon humor in this case, don't we?

COOKIE. (*In pain, as SHE tries to sit.*) Ahhhh!

WELCH. You hurtin' too, m'am?

COOKIE. Oh, I have a chronic back spasm. It's very hard for me to sit, stand or walk.

WELCH. And you didn't hear the gunshots either, I suppose?

COOKIE. No. I was dancing.

(WELCH looks at her in disbelief.)

COOKIE. Dancing is good for my back.

WELCH. And to think I was almost out the door with this one. (*To Chris*.) Mrs. Gorman?

CHRIS. Is that me? (*Looks around*.) Yes. Mrs. Gorman. Right.

WELCH. And what do you do?

CHRIS. Well, mostly, I've been helping with the drinks.

WELCH. Your occupation!

CHRIS. Oh, nothing ... No, not nothing. Well, I'm a liar – a lawyer! ... Sorry. ... And I'm a mother. I have two children. ... A boy ... No, one child ... Sorry. I'm very nervous.

WELCH. You and everybody else, m'am. I'm going to say something now that is not really a part of my official capacity. But I don't believe one God damn thing I've heard in this room. I think there were gunshots here tonight. I think someone or *everyone* is trying to cover up something. A man gets hit in the nose, another man stabs himself with a fork, someone's BMW gets smashed up, the host takes a short-legged dog for a walk and then goes to sleep, the hostess takes her father to a hospital in California with a broken hip, and nobody hears two gunshots because everybody is dancing, including a woman named Cookie who's been cooking all night who can't stand or walk! You people have to deal with me. I'm a real cop, you understand? I'm not somebody named Elmer that your kids watch on the Disney Channel . . . Now, I want some *real* answers, intelligent answers, believable answers, and answers that don't make me laugh. But first, I want to see Mr. Charley Brock and find out what the hell's going on here – including the possibility of him having two bullet holes in him. Now, I'll give you five seconds to get him down here, or I'll take two seconds and go upstairs and find him.

(*KEN and GLENN argue silently behind Welch's back.*)

WELCH. Don't mess with me now. I'm so close to a promotion, I can smell it. And I'm not going to screw it up with *this* case ... Do I start counting or do I start climbing up steps? It's up to you.

(*NOBODY moves. WELCH starts up the steps.*)

GLENN. Okay, just wait, will you? Wait a second. Wait. Okay? Can you wait? Just wait ... Ernie! Ken! I mean Len. I think it's time to call Charley and ask him to come down, don't you?
ERNIE. Definitely.
KEN. Absolutely.

(*ERNIE goes to the phone and rings Charley's room.*)

ERNIE. ... Charley? ... It's Ernie. We're ready for you now ... Are you ready for us now? ... Relax, Charley, that's just an hysteric nerve reaction.
KEN. What's wrong with him?
ERNIE. (*To Ken.*) He thinks he went temporarily blind. (*Into phone.*) Just put some cold water on your eyes and come down. There are two police officers who want to speak to you ... Why? ... BECAUSE YOU PUT OUT ONE FINGER, THAT'S WHY!! (*Hanging up and smiling at Welch.*) He's fine. He's coming down.
GLENN. The truth is, Officer, we were trying to protect Mr. Brock because he's a dear friend of ours. But we

know we're all in jeopardy if we hold back the truth. (*Crossing away from Welch.*) There *were* two gunshots here tonight. I, personally, did not hear them, but I share equal blame with those who *did* hear the shots and did not come forth with that information ... despite the fact that I didn't hear them.

KEN. Stop helping so much, Glenn.

GLENN. Nevertheless, Mr. Brock is willing to tell us the full and complete story, the details of which none of us has heard yet. About the missing help, about the disappearance of his wife, Myra, and about the two gunshots, which I didn't hear.

COOKIE. Oh, God, I'm getting another spasm in my back.

CHRIS. Oh, who gives a shit?

(*Charley's bedroom door opens. LENNY stands there as Charley, wearing a robe, pajamas and slippers, and a large bandage over his ear. THEY ALL look at him. HE looks at them, furious for making him do this.*)

GLENN. Hello, Charley.
KEN. Hi, Charley.
ERNIE. Feeling all right, Charley?

(*LENNY comes slowly down the stairs.*)

WELCH. I'm Officer Welch, Mr. Brock. This is Officer Pudney. Please sit down.

(*LENNY sits.*)

WELCH. Take this down, Connie.

(*SHE takes out her notebook.*)

WELCH. Now, Mr. Brock, tell us from the beginning
exactly what happened in this house tonight.
COOKIE. Does anyone want lemon tarts?
LENNY. Yes, a tart would be wonderful.
WELCH. Not now, m'am ... Go ahead, Mr. Brock.
LENNY. Okay ... Let's see ... the story ... as it
happened ... as I remember it ... as I'm telling it ... oh,
God ... Well, here goes . . . At exactly six o'clock tonight
I came home from work. My wife, Myra, was in her
dressing room getting dressed for the party. I got a bottle of
champagne from the refrigerator and headed upstairs.
Rosita, the Spanish cook, was in the kitchen with
Ramona, her Spanish sister and Romero, her Spanish son.
They were preparing an Italian dinner. They were waiting
for Myra to tell her when to start the dinner. As I climbed
the stairs, I said to myself, "It's my tenth wedding
anniversary and I can't believe I still love my wife so
much." Myra was putting on the perfume I bought her for
Christmas. I purposely buy it because it drives me crazy ...
I tapped on her door. Tap tap tap. She opens it. I hand her a
glass of champagne. I make a toast. (*Looking at Claire.*)
"To the most beautiful wife a man ever had for ten years."
She says, "To the best man and the best ten years a
beautiful wife ever had" ... We drink. We kiss. We toast
again. "To the loveliest skin on the loveliest body that has
never aged a day in ten wonderful years" ... She toasts, "To
the gentlest hands that ever stroked the loveliest skin that
never has aged in ten wonderful years" ... We drink. We
kiss. We toast ... We drink. We kiss. We toast ... By seven
o'clock the bottle is finished, my wife is sloshed and I'm

completely toasted ... And then I smell the perfume. The
perfume I could never resist ... I loved her in that moment
with as much passion and ardor as the night we were first
newlyweds. (*Rising. To Welch.*) I tell you this, not with
embarrassment, but with pride and joy for a love that
grows stronger and more lasting as each new day passes.
We lay there spent, naked in each other's arms, complete in
our happiness. It's now eight o'clock and outside it's
grown dark. Suddenly, a gentle knock on the door. Knock
knock knock. The door opens and a strange young man
looks down at us with a knife in his hands. Myra screams.
(*HE begins to act out the story.*) I jump up and run for the
gun in my drawer. Myra grabs a towel and shields herself. I
rush back in with the pistol, ready to save my wife's life.
The strange young man says in Spanish, "Yo quito se
dablo enchilada por quesa in quinto minuto." But I don't
speak Spanish and I never saw Rosita's son, Romero,
before, and I didn't know the knife was to cut up the salad
and he was asking should they heat up the dinner now? So
I aimed my gun at him, Myra screams and pulls my arm.
The gun goes off and shoots me in the ear lobe. Rosita's
son, Romero, runs downstairs and tells Rosita and
Ramona, "Mamasetta! Meela que paso el hombre ay baco
ay yah. El hombre que loco, que bang-bang"—the crazy
man took a shot at him. So, Rosita, Ramona and Romero
leave in a huff. My ear lobe is bleeding all over Myra's
new dress. Suddenly we hear a car pull up. It's the first
guests. Myra grabs a bathrobe and runs downstairs to stop
Rosita, Ramona and Romero, otherwise we'll have no
dinner. But they drive off in their Alfa Romeo. I look out
the window, but it's dark and I think someone is stealing
my beautiful old Mercedes, so I take another shot at them.
Myra runs down to the basement where we keep the cedar

chest. She's looking for the dress she wore last year for
Bonds for Israel. She can't find the light, trips down the
stairs, passes out in the dark. I run downstairs looking for
Myra, notice the basement door is open and afraid the
strange-looking kid is coming back, so I lock the door, not
knowing that Myra is still down there. Then I run upstairs
to take some aspirin because my ear lobe is killing me
from the hole in it. But the blood on my fingers gets in
my eyes and by mistake I take four Valium instead. I hear
the guests downstairs and I want to tell them to look for
Myra. But suddenly, I can't talk from the Valium, and I'm
bleeding on the white rug. So I start to write a note
explaining what happened, but the note looks like
gibberish. And I'm afraid they'll think it was a suicide note
and they'll call the police and my friend Glenn Cooper was
coming it would be very bad for his campaign to get mixed
up with a suicide, so I tore up the note and flushed it down
the toilet, just as they walked into my room. They're
yelling at me, "What happened? What happened?" And
before I could tell them what happened, I passed out on the
bed. And that's the whole goddam story, as sure as my
name is ... (*HE opens his robe to expose the monogram
"CB" on the pajamas.*) ... Charley Brock.

WELCH. (*Crossing to Lenny.*) I buy it. I buy the
whole thing. You know why I buy it? I buy it because I
liked it! I didn't *believe* it, but I liked it! I love my wife,
too, and that's why I want to get home early ... (*Crossing
to the front door.*) ... Sorry to bother you, folks. Take care
of that ear, Mr. Brock, and happy anniversary.

(*WELCH and PUDNEY leave. The OTHERS turn and
    look at Lenny.*)

GLENN. Where – where in the whole wide world did you find the guts to tell a story like that?

LENNY. (*Beaming.*) I made it up.

KEN. Of *course* you made it up. But when?

LENNY. As I was telling it. Sentence by sentence. Word by word. I didn't know where the hell I was going, but I just kept going.

(*We hear the POLICE CAR drive away.*)

CLAIRE. You don't even speak Spanish.

LENNY. I made the Spanish up, too.

CHRIS. You shit, we all could have gone to jail for perjury.

LENNY. (*Smiling.*) I know. That was the challenge. The ultimate chutzpah. It was the best goddam time I ever had in my life.

ERNIE. I am impressed. I am sincerely and deeply impressed. You have, without a doubt, Lenny, one of the weirdest minds I've ever come across.

CLAIRE. (*Holding up her glass.*) A toast to my husband, Lenny. Just when I was getting bored with our marriage, I fell in love with him all over again.

EVERYBODY. To Lenny!

CHRIS. I have an interesting question.

COOKIE. What?

CHRIS. What do you think really happened to Charley and Myra?

(*The INTERCOM buzzes.*)

ERNIE. (*Picks it up.*) Hello? ... Yes, Charley ... We're all here ... Are you up to having some visitors? ...

Wonderful ... We're dying to hear the story. We're on the way. (*HE hangs up.*) Charley is going to tell us the entire story.

(*THEY ALL begin to troop upstairs.*)

CHRIS. I hope it's shorter than Lenny's story.
CASSIE. (*To Glenn.*) Can we go back later and look for my crystal, honey?
GLENN. I'll buy you a thousand crystals, angel.

(*THEY are ALL on the stairs. Suddenly, we hear a KNOCK from inside the basement door. ALL stop and turn.*)

MYRA. (*From behind the door.*) Open the door. Open the door. Let me out!
KEN. Who is it?
MYRA. (*From behind the door.*) It's Myra!

(*THEY ALL look at Lenny is disbelief.*)

CURTAIN

COSTUME PLOT

LENNY

T-shirt
White dress shirt w/ dark stripes
Red bow tie
Red cummerbund
White suspenders
Studs & cufflinks
Black shoes
Black socks
Wedding ring
Wrist watch

Lt. Blue pajamas w/monogram
Rust robe

Brown slippers
Tape for ear bandage

KEN

T-shirt
Black tux w/vest
White dress shirt w/small bloodstain
Black bow tie
White suspenders
Black shoes
Black socks
Studs & cufflinks
Wedding ring
Wrist watch

GLENN

T-shirt
Black tux
Black bow tie
Black cummerbund
White suspenders
Black dress shoes
Black socks
White handkerchief
Studs & cufflinks
Watch

Bloody shirt
Bloody handkerchief

ERNIE

T-shirt
Black, Shawl collar old-style tux
White dress shirt
Black bow tie
Black cummerbund
White suspenders
Black dress shoes
Black socks
Studs & cufflinks
Wedding ring
Wrist watch

Black striped apron
Finger bandages

WELCH

Round-necked T-shirt
Blue policeman's uniform w/sleeve patch, badge & collar
    numbers
Navy uniform pants
Policeman's hat w/badge
Black belt
Black lace-up shoes
Black socks
Black watch
Gun belt w/holster, gun & handcuffs

CLAIRE

Off-black hose
Black panties
Black merry widow
Black & white re-embroidered lace dress
Black & rhinestone earrings
Rhinestone bracelet
Black evening bag w/zipper
Black dress shoes
Wedding ring
Dress watch

CHRIS

Off-black hose
Waist-nipper bra
Black briefs
Pink & black polka dot dress

Rhinestone earrings
Rhinestone bracelet
Black shoes
Black watch
Wedding ring

COOKIE

Hose
Green georgette slip
Green painted dress w/bead trim
Cinnabar necklace
Cinnabar bracelet
Pearl & ruby earrings
Gold mesh evening bag w/long chain
Gold shoes

Apron
Improvised gauze bandage

CASSIE

Nude hose
Black velvet sheath w/feathers
Black satin jacket
Black bead/crystal necklace
Rhinestone earrings
Wide rhinestone bracelet
Black satin shoes
Black satin clutch bag w/crystal
Wedding rings

Duplicate black jacket —distressed

PUDNEY

Blue policewoman's uniform w/patch, badge & collar
    numbers
Navy uniform pants
Policewoman's hat w/badge
Black belt
Black work shoes
Black socks
Black watch
Gun belt w/gun, holster, handcuffs, walkie-talkie, notepad

PROPERTY PLOT

Telephone table
Love seat
Two stacking tables
End tables
Two wooden armchairs w/upholstered seats
Sofa
Sofa end table
Coffee table w/glass top
Bar unit
Wooden chair w/upholstered seat
Wooden armchair w/upholstered seat (Upstairs bedroom)
Stereo cabinet
Tall table (DL)
Curio cabinet (upstairs landing)

Working Props:

Telephone w/long cord
Brass ashtray (on coffee table)
Sm. cigarette box w/5 cigarettes (coffee table)
Two books (sofa end table)
Top of bar:
    (4) rocks glasses
    (4) tumblers
    (1) ice bucket (empty)
    (1) vodka bottle (full)
    (1) gin bottle (full)
    (1) whiskey bottle (full)
    (1) ornate decanter

Inside bar cabinet:

(4) cans Coke
glasses and bottles as dressing

On stereo cabinet:
    (5) cigarettes in large cigarette box

On tall table (DL):
    (1) glass ashtray
    (1) cigarette lighter

In Charley's bedroom:
    (1) first aid kit (sealed shut)
    (1) blue hand towel

In guest bedroom:
    (1) white hand towel

On stage right prop table:
    (1) Steuben gift box w/broken glass (Lenny)
    (1) black clutch purse (Claire)
    (1) magenta gift box (Ernie)
    (1) sausage cushion (Cookie)
    (1) gold purse (Cookie)
    (1) tall trash can (Ernie)
    (1) silver gift box (Glenn)
    (1) walkie-talkie (Pudney)
    (2) guns w/holsters (Welch & Pudney)
    (2) pads w/pens (Welch & Pudney)

On stage left prop table:
    (1) pretzel bag (Lenny)
    (2) glasses w/plastic ice (Claire)
    (9) plastic ice cubes (Chris)

(1) tumbler w/spritzer & plastic ice (Ernie)
(1) tumbler w/Perrier & lime & plastic ice (Ernie)
(1) Rocks glass w/double scotch & plastic ice (Ernie)
(1) roll paper towels (Ernie)
(2) unopened champagne bottles (Ernie)
(6) china plates (Cookie)
(1) ladle (Cookie)
(1) blue ice bag (Cookie)
(1) rice dish w/spoon (Cookie)
(1) improvised gauze bandage (Cookie)
(4) unbreakable plates (Ernie)

Working props Act II

Telephone (on DR stacking table)
On sofa end table:
    (1) plate w/food remnants & napkin
    (1) empty wine glass
    (1) empty wine bottle
    (1) empty coffee mug

On wooden armchair (SR):
    (1) sausage cushion
    (1) plate w/food remnants & napkin

On wooden chair (RC):

    (1) plate w/edible food remnants & napkin

On coffee table:
    (1) empty champagne bottle
    (2) plates w/food remnants & napkins
    (2) empty coffee mugs

(1) duck carcass on platter
(1) rocks glass w/scotch
(1) Coke can 1/2 full
(1) brass ashtray
(1) baggie w/plastic ice
(1) bowl w/noodles
(1) small cigarette box
(1) empty wine bottle

On sofa end table:
(1) empty plate w/food remnants & napkin
(2) empty champagne glass
(2) empty coffee cups

On bar cabinet:
(1) plate w/food remnants & napkin
(1) wooden tray w/espresso samovar, (6) demitasse cups, saucers, spoons, creamer, sugar bowl
(4) rocks glasses
(4) tumblers
(1) ice bucket
(1) Coke can
(1) vodka bottle (full)
(1) gin bottle (full)
(1) whiskey bottle (full)
(1) decorative decanter

On stereo cabinet:
(1) large cigarette box w/(5) cigarettes
(1) lighter
(1) sm. ashtray
(1) empty champagne bottle

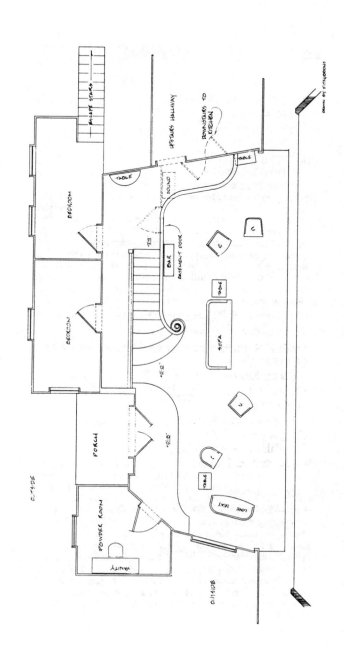

WHAT THE BELLHOP SAW
(Little Theatre)
(FARCE)

by Wm. Van Zandt and Jane Milmore

8 male, 4 female

The play starts with a rather nice fellow checking into a
$400.00 suite in "New York City's finest hotel". From there it
snowballs into a fabulous nightmare involving a Salman
Rushdie-type author, an Iranian Terrorist, a monstrous shrew-
like woman, a conniving bellboy, a monumentally
incompetent F.B.I. man, a nubile celebrity-mad maid, a dim-
witted secretary, and a cute little pigtailed girl. All the while,
gag lines are popping at Orville Redenbacher speed.
Everything happens at pretty much whirlwind velocity. This
latest farce by Van Zandt and Milmore combines topical humor
with the traditional antics of farce: doors slamming,
characters careening and confusion reigning supreme.   A
wildly funny farce! An excellent piece of workmanship by our
two authors who take pride in the old-fashioned craft of
comedy writing. #25062

◆◆◆◆◆◆◆◆◆◆◆◆◆◆◆◆◆◆◆◆◆◆◆◆◆◆◆◆◆◆◆◆

THE SENATOR WORE PANTYHOSE
(Little Theatre)
(COMEDY)

by Wm. Van Zandt and Jane Milmore

7 male, 3 female

If you're tired of political and religious scandals, this is your
greatest revenge!   Van Zandt & Milmore's latest comedy
revolves around the failing Presidential campaign of "Honest"
Gabby Sandalson, a regular guy whose integrity has all but
crippled his bid for the White House. Desparate for votes, his
sleazeball campaign manager trumps up an implausible sex
scandal which accidentally backfires on PMS Club leader
Reverend Johnny and his makeup-faced wife Honey Pie; an
opportunistic innkeeper with a penchant for antique food; the
town's wayward single girl; two escaped convicts looking for
stolen loot; and newscaster Don Bother. "A guaranteed hit!"
(Asbury Park Press) "The characters swap beds, identities and
jabs in what may be a flawless sex farce." (The Register).
#21084

MIXED FEELINGS
(Little Theatre—Comedy)

Donald Churchill
m., 2 f., Int.

This is a riotous comedy about divorce, that ubiquitous, peculiar institution which so shapes practically everyone's life. Arthur and Norma, ex-spouses, live in separate apartments in the same building. Norma has second thoughts about her on-going affair with Arthur's best-friend; while Arthur isn't so sure he wants to continue *his* dalliance with Sonia, wife of a manufacturer with amusingly kinky sexual tastes (Dennis—the manufacturer—doesn't mind that his wife is having an affair; just so long as she continues to provide him with titillating accounts of it while he is dressed as a lady traffic cop). Most of Sonia's accounts are pure fiction, which seems to keep Dennis happy. Comic sparks are ignited into full-fledged farcical flames in the second act, when Dennis arrives in Arthur's flat for lessons in love from the legendary Arthur! "Riotous! A domestic laught romp! A super play. You'll laugh all the way home, I promise you.'—Eastbourne News. "Very funny ... a Churchill comedy that most people will thoroughly enjoy."—The Stage. Restricted New York City.

THE DECORATOR
(Little Theatre/Comedy)

Donald Churchill
m., 2 f., Int.

Much to her surprise, Marcia returns home to find that her flat has not been painted, as she arranged. In fact, the job hasn't even been started yet. There on the premises is the housepainter who is filling in for his ill colleague. As he begins work, there is a surprise visitor--the wife of the man with whom Marcia is having an affair, who has come to confront her nemesis and to exact her revenge by informing Marcia's husband of his wife's infidelity. Marcia is at her wit's end about what to do, until she gets a brilliant idea. It seems the housepainter is a part-time professional actor. Marcia hires him to impersonate her husband, Reggie, at the big confrontation later that day, when the wronged wife plans to return and spill the beans. Hilarity is piled upon hilarity as the housepainter, who takes his acting *very* seriously, portrays the absent Reggie. The wronged wife decides that the best way to get back at Marcia would be to sleep with her "husband" (the house painter), which is an ecstatic experience for them both. When Marcia learns that the housepainter/actor/husband has slept with her rival, she demands to have the opportunity to show the housepainter what *really* good sex is. "This has been the most amazing day of my life", says the sturdy painter, as Marcia leads him into her bedroom. "Irresistible."—London Daily Telegraph.

LEND ME A TENOR
(Farce)
by KENNETH LUDWIG

4 male, 4 female

This is the biggest night in history of the Cleveland Grand Opera Company, for this night in September, 1934, world-famous tenor Tito Morelli (also known as "Il Stupendo") is to perform his greatest role ("Otello") at the gala season-opening benefit performance which Mr. Saunders, the General Manager, hopes will put Cleveland on the operatic map. Morelli is late in arriving--and when he finally sweeps in, it is too late to rehearse with the company. Through a wonderfully hilarious series of mishaps, Il Stupendo is given a double dose of tranquilizers which, mixed with all the booze he has consumed, causes him to pass out. His pulse is so low that Saunders and his assistant, Max, believe to their horror that he has died. What to do? What to do? Max is an aspiring singer, and Saunders persuades him to black up, get into Morelli's Otello costume, and try to fool the audience into thinking that's Il Stupendo up there. Max succeeds admirably, but the comic sparks really fly when Morelli comes to and gets into his other costume. Now we have *two* Otellos running around, in costume, and two women running around, in lingerie -- each thinking she is with Il Stupendo! A sensation on Broadway and in London's West End. "A jolly play."--NY Times. "Non-stop laughter"--Variety. "Uproarious! Hysterical!"--USA Today. "A rib-tickling comedy."--NY Post. (#667) Posters.

POSTMORTEM
(Thriller)
by KENNETH LUDWIG

4 male, 4 female . Int..

Famous actor-manager and playwright William Gillette, best known for over a generation as Sherlock Holmes in his hugely-successful adaptation of Conan Doyle (which is *still* a popular play in the Samuel French Catalogue), has invited the cast of his latest revival of the play up for a weekend to his home in Connecticut, a magnificent pseudo-medieval, Rhenish castle on a bluff overlooking the Connecticut River. Someone is trying to murder William Gillette, and he has reason to suspect that it is one of his guests for the weekend. Perhaps the murderer is the same villain who did away with Gillette's fiancee a year ago if you believe, as does Gillette, that her death was not--as the authorities concluded--a suicide. Gillette's guests include his current ingenue/leading lady and her boyfriend, his Moriarty and his wife, and Gillette's delightfully acerbic sister. For the evening's entertainment Gillette has arranged a seance, conducted by the mysterious Louise Perradine, an actress twenty years before but now a psychic medium. The intrepid and more than slightly eccentric William Gillette has taken on, in "real life", his greatest role: he plans to solve the case *a la* Sherlock Holmes! The seance is wonderfully eerie, revealing one guest's closely-guarded secret and sending another into hysterics, another into a swoon, as Gillette puts all the pieces of the mystery together before the string of attempts on his life leads to a rousingly melodramatic finale. " shots in the dark and darkly held secrets, deathbed letters, guns and knives and bottles bashed over the head, ghosts and hiders behind curtains and misbegotten suspicions. There are moments when you'll jump. Guaranteed."--The Telegraph. (#18677)

THE GOOD DOCTOR

NEIL SIMON

(All Groups) Comedy
2 Men, 3 Women. Various settings.

With Christopher Plummer in the role of the Writer, we are introduced to a composite of Neil Simon and Anton Chekhov, from whose short stories Simon adapted the capital vignettes of this collection. Frances Sternhagen played, among other parts, that of a harridan who storms a bank and upbraids the manager for his gout and lack of money. A father takes his son to a house where he will be initiated into the mysteries of sex, only to relent at the last moment, and leave the boy more perplexed than ever. In another sketch a crafty seducer goes to work on a wedded woman, only to realize that the woman has been in command from the first overture. Let us not forget the classic tale of a man who offers to drown himself for three rubles. The stories are droll, the portraits affectionate, the humor infectious, and the fun unending.

"As smoothly polished a piece of work as we're likely to see all season."—*N.Y. Daily News.* "A great deal of warmth and humor —vaudevillian humor—in his retelling of these Chekhovian tales."—*Newhouse Newspapers.* "There is much fun here . . . Mr. Simon's comic fancy is admirable."—*N.Y. Times.*

(Music available. Write for particulars.)

The Prisoner of Second Avenue

NEIL SIMON

(All Groups) Comedy
2 Men, 4 Women, Interior

Mel is a well-paid executive of a fancy New York company which has suddenly hit the skids and started to pare the payroll. Anxiety doesn't help; Mel, too, gets the ax. His wife takes a job to tide them over, then she too is sacked. As if this weren't enough, Mel is fighting a losing battle with the very environs of life. Polluted air is killing everything that grows on his terrace; the walls of the high-rise apartment are paper-thin, so that the private lives of a pair of German stewardesses next door are open books to him; the apartment is burgled; and his psychiatrist dies with $23,000 of his money. Mel does the only thing left for him to do: he has a nervous breakdown. It is on recovery that we come to esteem him all the more. For Mel and his wife and people like them have the resilience, the grit to survive.

"Now all this, mind you, is presented primarily in humorous terms."—*N.Y. Daily News.* "A gift for taking a grave subject and, without losing sight of its basic seriousness, treating it with hearty but sympathetic humor . . . A talent for writing a wonderfully funny line . . . full of humor and intelligence . . . Fine fun."—*N.Y. Post.* "Creates an atmosphere of casual cataclysm, and everyday urban purgatory of copelessness from which laughter seems to be released like vapor from the city's manholes."—*Time.*

Other Publications for Your Interest

NOISES OFF

(LITTLE THEATRE—FARCE)

By MICHAEL FRAYN

5 men, 4 women—2 Interiors

This wonderful Broadway smash hit is "a farce about farce, taking the clichés of the genre and shaking them inventively through a series of kaleidoscopic patterns. Never missing a trick, it has as its first act a pastiche of traditional farce; as its second, a contemporary variant on the formula; as its third, an elaborate undermining of it. The play opens with a touring company dress-rehearsing 'Nothing On', a conventional farce. Mixing mockery and homage, Frayn heaps into this play-within-a-play a hilarious melee of stock characters and situations. Caricatures—cheery char, outraged wife and squeaky blonde—stampede in and out of doors. Voices rise and trousers fall . . . a farce that makes you think as well as laugh."—London Times Literary Supplement. ". . . as side-splitting a farce as I have seen. Ever? *Ever.*"—John Simon, NY Magazine. "The term 'hilarious' must have been coined in the expectation that something on the order of this farce-within-a-farce would eventually come along to justify it."—N.Y. Daily News. "Pure fun."—N.Y. Post. "A joyous and loving reminder that the theatre really does go on, even when the show falls apart."—N.Y. Times.   (#16052)

THE REAL THING

(ADVANCED GROUPS—COMEDY)

By TOM STOPPARD

4 men, 3 women—Various settings

The effervescent Mr. Stoppard has never been more intellectually—and *emotionally*—engaging than in this "backstage" comedy about a famous playwright named Henry Boot whose second wife, played on Broadway to great acclaim by Glenn Close (who won the Tony Award), is trying to merge "worthy causes" (generally a euphemism for left-wing politics) with her art as an actress. She has met a "political prisoner" named Brodie who has been jailed for radical thuggery, and who has written an inept play about how property is theft, about how the State stifles the Rights of The Individual, etc., etc., etc. Henry's wife wants him to make the play work theatrically, which he does after much soul-searching. Eventually, though, he is able to convince his wife that Brodie is emphatically *not* a victim of political repression. He is, in fact, a *thug.* Famed British actor Jeremy Irons triumphed in the Broadway production (Tony Award), which was directed to perfection by none other than Mike Nichols (Tony Award). "So densely and entertainingly packed with wit, ideas and feelings that one visit just won't do . . . Tom Stoppard's most moving play and the most bracing play anyone has written about love and marriage in years."—N.Y. Times. "Shimmering, dazzling theatre, a play of uncommon wit and intelligence which not only thoroughly delights but challenges and illuminates our lives."—WCBS-TV. 1984 Tony Award-Best Play.   (#941)